"[*Daniel Fights a Hurricane*] reads like if Franz Kafka and Anne Carson got together and re-wrote *The Wizard of Oz*, with occasional in-text illustrations by Dave Eggers... A surreal and playful postmodern fable about an epic struggle against a villainous force-of-nature, with a surprisingly human love story of intriguing complexity."
—W MAGAZINE

"Filled with surreal, hallucinogenic imagery ranging from the terrifying to the hilarious."
—THE AWL

"A wild book full of brain-consuming storms and jacked-up teeth and mysterious tigers and breakfast at McDonald's. While so many other books and movies these days seem to be afraid of their own fantasies, Shane Jones goes for the throat. Fans of his previous novel, *Light Boxes*, or who like Donald Antrim or Kelly Link or, I don't know, Buñuel, can expect a black, fun freakshow."
—VICE

"A joy to read... Gentle, quirky and ultimately redeeming... A marvelous melding of metaphor and reality."
—SHELF AWARENESS

"A bewitching new novel... It's Jones' juxtaposition of the fantastical and, say, a woman polishing off a McDonald's Sausage McMuffin that makes his work feel so unique."
—NYLON

"Shane Jones' latest novel *Daniel Fights a Hurricane* magnetizes the eye to its watercolor collision course. It's a lighthearted, good-natured tragedy powdered with bubbles, feathers, shaggy-haired rock gardens and folded kangaroos. It's playful enough to hold court in the camp of anti-pretentiousness, yet so sad and demented that even the anthropomorphic 'bears throwing acorns like grenades at squirrels' add an air of menace."
—THE TOTTENVILLE REVIEW

"Playful and dreamlike, the true, the imagined, and the truly-imagined swirl together to create, yes, a hurricane of a world that will suck you in and offer little hope of escape."
—FLAVORPILL, "10 NEW MUST READS FOR JULY"

"Shane Jones is a serious player in the world of playfully serious fiction. Better start reading him now."
—SAM LIPSYTE, AUTHOR OF *HOME LAND* AND *THE ASK*

"Shane Jones takes the strands of dreams and reality and combines them so inextricably that it forms the DNA of an entirely new and wonderful species."
—KEVIN WILSON, AUTHOR OF *THE FAMILY FANG*

"A dream in the land of Brautigan written on the interior of a welding mask for proper pipemaking."
—JESSE BALL, AUTHOR OF *THE CURFEW* AND *SAMEDI THE DEAFNESS*

"A quietly deft and linguistically playful book about the struggle between so-called reality and the realities of the imagination. *Daniel Fights a Hurricane* is about the way realities cross, collide, and twine around each other, and the lives that are wounded by being caught in between."
—BRIAN EVENSON, AUTHOR OF *FUGUE STATE*

Crystal Eaters

SHANE JONES

TWO DOLLAR RADIO
Books too loud to ignore.

TWO DOLLAR RADIO is a family-run outfit founded in 2005 with the mission to reaffirm the cultural and artistic spirit of the publishing industry.

We aim to do this by presenting bold works of literary merit, each book, individually and collectively, providing a sonic progression that we believe to be too loud to ignore.

Cover: Dannemora mine with the open pit "Storrymningen,"
Elias Martin, 1780-1800.
Author photograph: Erin Pihlaja

Typeset in Garamond, the best font ever.
Printed in the United States of America.

TWO DOLLAR RADIO
Books too loud to ignore.

www.TwoDollarRadio.com
twodollar@TwoDollarRadio.com

Crystal Eaters

Part One

40

It feels good to believe in one hundred.

They walk through the village wondering how many they have left. Their land is homes and shacks lining seven dirt roads. Everything is hit with sun. Tin roofs glare. Wooden structures glow. The city appeared at the horizon like a mountain range decades ago but it's close now – dangerously close and growing closer by the day – and believing in one hundred is a distraction. A long road connects the village to the crystal mine. A man named Z. mumbles his number and walks by the home of Remy.

Inside Remy's home Harvak the dog is on the table. With each breath his stomach balloons pink skin. His left eye drips crystal (Chapter 5, Death Movement, Book 8) and his count lowers. Remy thinks about lying face down and entering a place where she wouldn't hurt. She pets Harvak's head ten times but nothing happens. She touches a Harvak hair on his leg longer than the rest. When she pulls the hair like a rope attached to an anchor, fingers over fingers instead of hand over hand, the end result is a hole with zero inside. She spins the hair into a wreath. With one finger she taps the hole ten times but again nothing happens.

Two gasps from Harvak are split by Dad yelling from downstairs that dinner is ready. Her hand bleeds from Harvak's teeth. His body stiffens with cooled blood and fleas jump from the remaining fur so she covers him with the blue sheet and places the hair wreath on top.

Harvak lost his count in various ways.

One afternoon in the crystal mine he slipped, kind of toppled forward over his own front legs and fell down a sharp incline, jaw spooning black dirt outward, spine struggling to right itself with twists.

Remy accidently hit him with her bike and the snap, like a tree branch, made Remy look to the woods, not back at her dog with the broken leg twitching in the road.

The most damaging was the village-wide panic when the city came into focus, shadow-bodies grazing on the horizon. Everyone went into a panic, filling burlap sacks with canned goods and clothing, quickly clearing shelves. They sprinted from their homes after double-locking their doors with two-by-fours, and they slept in tents in the mine. Elders said to protect the crystals. Some held knives. The strongest took turns patrolling the perimeter, resting against the stilts of wooden structures while others read books and played a game where they tossed crystals into cardboard boxes from fifty feet away. What they forgot was Harvak. It was deemed too dangerous to return. Late at night Remy tried to sneak out and was restrained, full nelson, by a boy with a black facial scar in the shape of a key who told her the city is coming, get into the mine and hide. Harvak stayed pressed against a window where he waited for an approaching body, no food or water near, the sun warming the glass. Remy imagined his ribs rising through his fur.

Other punishments included being slapped for eating Dad's boots. Put in a room for barking he couldn't control because he was scared of the city. Screamed at for running in the house and wobbling a lamp that tilted the light from Mom who had fallen asleep on the couch holding a red box. Punishments created by humans and placed on dogs. Remy's dog. Her dog. Harvak.

Looking at the blue sheet's shape on the table she pulls herself through every negative moment resulting in a lower number. Harvak is far past the life expectancy of a dog (40 crystals) and his old age has quickly taken the remainder in the last week.

Remy asked her parents before if crystals could be added, life extended. Dad said no with the word tucked inside a breath over his forked potato. With the simplest questions Remy felt like she was bothering him. Mom said yellow were used for electricity, blue were common, red and green rare, and don't mention black, because despite the rumors no one's seen one. You can't increase your count because your number only knows how to get smaller.

"Dinner," Dad repeats from the kitchen, his voice hard, angry.

Remy once believed each pet on Harvak produced one crystal inside. Every day, falling asleep in bed, she made sure to touch him a minimum of ten times. She's done this to herself before, while standing at the bathroom mirror, tapping her body in sets of ten, starting at her forehead, then to her shoulders, then to her heart, and finally ending at her stomach where the crystals shine.

If I walked away, got in bed, got into a position where I couldn't see what was happening right now maybe my number wouldn't fall.

In the kitchen Remy says Harvak is gone. Under the amber ceiling light they stand. Dad leans against the sink, water running over wooden dishes. He exhales and stares at his boots. Something more than Harvak's death is wrong. There's silence and dread stacked on top of previous silence and dread. Mom says she's sorry into Remy's head. From Mom's mouth pressed into her hair Remy smells the sourness of dead dogs and she begins, with one finger, counting on Mom's back.

39

With lips coated in glittering filth, dressed in red shorts with white trim, Remy mourns Harvak's death by running like a dog in the crystal mine. Two separate roads – one for trucks to enter and one for them to exit – spiral down to a field with pyramids of excavated dirt. Remy as dog-child moves on all fours. On the dirt mine walls rest wooden buckets dangling from a pulley system built on the ground above. Idle work trucks with their gun metal paneling appear two-dimensional in the evening light glimmer while Remy's left hand shines wet with blood from the rocks that pinprick her palm.

She imagines her count as a loose pile of yellow in her belly, not a stack of a hundred red. No combination of touching her body helps, it just feels good.

As a toddler, lying in bed on top of the covers, naked, with blond hair hooked around her shoulders, she asked Mom to place a hand on her stomach and to guess how many. When her hand touched her skin Remy puffed her chest and made a scared inhale. Mom said *One hundred*. She asked Dad, who was in the garage fixing the truck, his head buried under the hood, if she'd reach a day when her count would be zero. He pulled himself from the engine holding a wrench the size of her forearm. He crouched with the wrench on his thigh. At first he seemed irritated because she had interrupted his work, but then he said *As long as your Mother is around you'll always have at least one.*

She knows now that everyone is losing.

Kids in the village have witnessed their parents vomiting blue and yellow slush into kitchen sinks, toilets, couch cushions, their laps. Remy has studied Mom's lead-heavy movements, her shortened steps, her cough that turns heads at the market. Remy can help herself and Mom by learning how to add crystals to what is already inside, she just needs to figure out how. There must be a way to add. There must be a way to reverse the fall. Like the thought that Brother rallied behind so obsessively and look where he is now, city prison. The universe is a system where children watch their parents die. Mom loses weight with sunsets. Her skin dims with sleep. Remy tells herself that she'll be the one to figure out what nobody else can. She'll save Mom from experiencing the number zero.

Dad's answer when asked what's wrong: *A disease has entered her and we can't get it out.*

Remy as dog-child rolls in the dirt. She runs on all fours toward a mine tunnel. The only color on Remy under the moonlight is her eyes and several streaks of blond hair the dirt hasn't covered. A man in the city stands at The Bend using binoculars. There are two other men, one on each side of the man, and they take turns passing the binoculars and laughing and drinking from tall moon-reflecting cans. Remy barks into the mine tunnel until her echo comes back.

38

It's difficult to move under the heat wave twisting the sky into something new. For weeks the temperature has only risen. There's no relief in the forecast.

The heat melted a green crystal. Z. smeared the green across his forehead and laughed from the shelling sensation on his skin as they walked the fence. So many men with long limbs and goofy faces. Their name is Brothers Feast, and according to Z., they will be remembered forever.

On both sides of the fence are enormous dirt fields. In the distance – the city and prison. Ricky heaves a bottle over the fence and they run in the dark, laughing, back to their humble homes so unlike the city's structures. They have technology. The village has crystals. Tendrils of turquoise from city pollution screen the moon above.

"We're going to be someone," says Z. "C-c-c-come on, back to the fence. B-b-b-back to looking at the prison."

The city is a weed. It grows closer with buildings being built and will soon cover the village. The elderly watch closely like they do the sun and they preach it's end times. Others believe the city moves because they want to destroy what is archaic. The village has nowhere to run. Their way of life doesn't match up with the city way of life. They are bigger. Here it all comes, they say. Open up, they say. We're fucked, they say.

The prison is located on an island of land built slightly away from the main city buildings, connected by a single-lane road.

"We'll be r-r-r-remembered," says Z. "Just you guys wait."

The lights illuminate curling barbed wire and concrete walls so tall and smooth the Brothers often ask each other during meetings *How did they build them so high without it collapsing? Is it magic? Must be magic.* The city is navy blue suits, cafeterias, ham sandwiches, granite counters, several types of stop signs, mouth-mint dentists, blacked-out car windows, bottled water, eight-to-six office jobs, drywall. But the prison is different, something special, like magic.

"Is anyone listening to me when I say g-g-g-great things will happen?" says Z. "Anyone, anyone at all?"

The Brothers answers yes, they know, great things are coming. They dream of prisoners running wild with guards trailing, the air above the guards' heads whisked with batons, lights exploding through their bodies, the air sticky and sweet with perimeter flowers blooming like smoke on the single-lane road as they run.

"Men have always been scared of the city, r-r-r-remember our lives in hiding. Depressing. We can't hide anymore, the city won't let us. Here it c-c-c-comes."

For inmates, the worst part isn't being locked up and having a shoebox-sized window to squeeze their face against, observing the city and imagining their loved ones eating cherry pie. The worst part is they can't see the beautiful place holding them. They can't see the lights spiking the night sky like Brothers Feast can, standing, at the fence.

"If you're remembered f-f-f-forever, you live f-f-f-forever."

The Brothers aren't listening. They can't concentrate on anything else beside the prison. They know Z. is talking, but they don't process what he's saying.

"Agree," someone says.

"Doing it," says another.

"The t-t-t-trick," says Z., "is to become part of p-p-p-peo-ple's memories, their reality."

37

Dog = 40
Ant = 3
Bird = 10
Mold = 678
Baby = 100
Mother's tear = half
Plant = 230
Remy = unknown
Cat = 39
Spit = partial
Cloud = 88
Horse = unknown
Moon = 4,000
Frog = 12
City = infinite
Village = always falling
Tree = 480
Fly = 4
Sun = 10,000
Rabbit = 8
Mirror = reflective of object
Dirt = infinite
Pinecone = 7
Lamb = 22
Air = infinite
Flower = 1

Crystal count is depleted gradually over time but can be drastically decreased by events. Getting hit by a truck would most likely erase a baby's one hundred. If the baby survived, wrapped in a tiny full-body cast, her count would be similar to a rabbit's. Her count would no longer be a shining triangle of one hundred perfectly stacked crystals inside her body because it would resemble scattered shale.

The village survives on myth.

There is the story of Royal Bob, a myth so old it is easily dismissed today, but a story that is still told. Royal Bob is the first person to find a black crystal. He boiled it down into dark syrup that he sipped for decades. Seen running at night in blue shorts, mouth open, grinning, head tilted back with his gray hair stretching twenty feet behind him, dogs weaving in and out. Royal Bob rarely spoke, never entered daylight, but the myth says he preached several times at night, in a mine tunnel lit with hanging lanterns, about the black crystal to the elderly. His body was never found. All the glass tubes were empty inside his home – the elderly slowly walking the halls, picking up the glass tubes by thumb and finger and dropping them into burlap sacks. Some say Royal Bob lives inside the mine where he runs endlessly through the tunnels. You can see his hair. Some say Royal Bob will never be zero because he's forever filled with black crystal. Some say his soul is tethered to the gravity of all village dirt. Others say he escaped into the city so he could destroy it. But no one knows because a myth is a myth.

The oldest books advise worshiping the crystals excavated from the mine. Today these practices are limited, deemed antiquated and pointless by many. Most crystals, especially red and green, are for selling now. The yellow are melted and poured through machines. Red crystals become knick-knacks displayed on tables and mantels. Few believe in their healing powers. But the mining still continues at a high rate, day and night, because it's what they've always done and they need the yellow (YCL) for their lamps, refrigerators, and generators.

Discussing your count in the village is like discussing the weather in the city.

Count is not a city belief. They want to take over the village. Those in the city have little understanding of the village and are comfortable with destroying it and capturing the crystal mine because it's all so different from their way of life. The city believes in the new ways of progress, not the old ways of tradition and simplicity. Many use The Bend not only as a curved road to jog, but to look in at the village and wonder why they live the way they do. They bring binoculars and get drunk and stare. Legislation has been passed to install high-powered stand-alone "binocular stations" costing taxpayers fifteen thousand dollars, including the salary of a part-time "binocular attendant" and not one complaint to date has been filed. The city lives like it will never die.

Remy spends hours touching her stomach, trying to predict her count. She wants a hundred crystals shining like a campfire. When she looks at herself in the bathroom mirror she only sees the dark and wonders if she'd be prettier if she lived in the city, had lipstick, dresses, shampoo infused with rose oil, sunglasses to cover her face.

Once, she saw green crystals in the corner of her eye. Four of them hung like beads of water from her eyelid and when she ran downstairs to show Mom they broke into a pea-green pool clouding her vision.

"I swear they were there."

"I know," said Mom, inspecting Remy's eye. It wouldn't stop blinking. "I've seen them before."

"Really?"

"As a baby they blinded you."

"Scary."

"The body is small then and the crystals are everywhere. Sometimes, they come out."

"And now they're gone?" said Remy. She touched her eye.

"And now," said Mom, pulling Remy's hand from her face, "they're gone."

She thinks about her parents, and Brother in prison, and wonders who is closest to exhaling their final crystal. Who will become a husk? Who will become zero? She thinks *Definitely Mom*. She thinks *Then Dad*. She thinks *Then just me filling up their space.*

Mom's illness diminishes Dad because he is helpless against it and is forced to fall back on vague coping mechanisms of, "She is sick and losing, and it's natural. Let the process be the process." He crushes everything inside. Emotion comes in outbursts, the occasional closed eyes and biting-his-bottom-lip while standing over the kitchen sink, washing dishes with the sun seeping in hot and ugly. Remy hates the way he moves through the house – slowly and with caution – as if he knows, selfishly, egotistically, that he's the one who will hear her last breath.

Dad shouted about count through every wall, floor, and ceiling in the house last night. "Doesn't she understand you start with a hundred and then you lose them," he said. Mom sat in bed, covered in dandelion-print sheets and used the spitting cloth to expel the color red. "It's simple," he said.

36

He keeps a box in the closet. The bottoms of hanging shirts cover the box like a hiding child. The box is white. Inside is a crystal with eight smooth sides, a sharp point, and a rough fire-burned looking end.

Gripping a sharpened spoon he uncurls a fingernail-sized piece from the black crystal. Tapping the edge with his thumb he makes sure there is a sharp edge to cut his mouth. More dangerous if the edge is dull.

He sits on his bed with the crystal floating in a pool of saliva beneath his tongue. His legs are splayed in a wide V. He throws himself back, aiming for the pillow, but bangs his head against the headboard. Moving the piece of crystal around the bottom of his mouth he inhales and exhales, feels a surge of expecting blood widening its cells. Sliding down on the bed he positions the pillow behind his head and gets ready.

Before the prison was erected there was a ribbon-cutting ceremony. There were pink-skinned politicians and a crowd of shoulder-shruggers and a pair of giant scissors an intern held for two hours. A politician named Sanders stood at a podium too short for his height and struggling to speak into the microphone said: "Ellsworth Correctional… we will treat inmates with respect and compassion here. They will live with minimal supervision. Cells will be similar to our own bedrooms at home. The idea is simple – those who break the law should be kept away from the general population, but in the community that lawbreakers create inside Ellsworth Correctional they should feel free and normal no matter if they are uneducated people with poor social skills." And then later, near the end of his speech: "Inmates are not animals!" The crowd cheered but they weren't sure what they were cheering for other than the sweaty enthusiasm of Sanders. Construction began immediately with men in orange hats and yellow machines zigzagging the grounds. Sanders pressed his suit jacket to his heart when a backhoe struck rock. For months the villagers watched the prison rise slowly, dangerously, blinking and craning their necks, wondering how something so large could be so real.

Head on pillow, box resting on his stomach, Pants McDonovan presses his tongue on the crystal until it's angled against his gums, aimed at the roots of his bottom front teeth. He grinds it in. Ringing his head, the tearing of cheesecloth. He sees himself as a child kissing Mom goodnight, Harvak barking, when the family was a family. He played spit-tag with Remy in the mine and jogged with Dad through the streets and the family glowed, discussed their day over plates of pork and carrots. Before bed, Dad poured YCL into the generator and he helped with little nervous hands because Dad always corrected him, always told him he was either pouring too fast or too slow, he wanted to get it right, he wanted to pour smoothly, and sometimes, he did, but Dad never noticed with Pants holding the bucket just so with his arms trembling. This was a time of worship and prayer. The sun didn't scream and spit a heat wave. The city was faraway and could be laughed at, could be mocked by thrusting your hips at it or turning and lowering your pants. He collected bugs in mason jars and hid them in his closet. He asked Mom for potted plants to be placed near his crystals. He wanted living things to always be in his room. At night he would listen to the bugs and position the plants in the moonlight.

Fire pools across his chest and drips from his ribs as he swallows. He sits up and inhales — eyes trying to escape from their sockets looking cartoonish — chest puffed in rash, arms stiff at his sides with fists punched into the mattress. His feet are numb with needles, but it's worth it. Going to come alive, going to balance out now. He leans over the bed and spits a stretched glob of sparkling blood on the cement floor.

A dirt cloud from clapped together shoes (Friday, Tony's job) floats by and a transparent Younger Mom hovers in the debris. She says hello then disappears, her gown becoming her then all becoming the dirt cloud becoming the air. Without moving his arm, hand at his side, he does a little wave.

More spit. The glob is a thick stream with no end. This is a reaction from eating black crystal that happens once every two hundred times. A cleansing. When the stream detaches from his mouth he falls to the floor and does 50 pushups — his ponytail wrapped around his neck hitting the floor before his chest. Turning his head, he spit-sprays the wall in the shape of Mom.

He stands. He touches the heat inside his forearms by way of his lips. His shirt, a ridiculously huge hand-me-down from Mom with a duck drawing that Dad once wore and made fun of, is saturated in sweat and he pulls the shirt off and whips it around his head before helicoptering it across the room. His right foot twists and slips left in blood.

He hits the peak.

Jogging in place, he imagines a sunset at his back and Harvak at his side. The black crystal is collapsing his veins. He runs his hand through the top of his buzz-cut before grabbing the rubber band holding his ponytail. Once pulled through he shakes his head and a flap of blond hair bounces off his upper back. He looks ridiculous and insane. He's on a beach telling the tide to wait. He's running from the smell of salt. The village is in the distance and there's a forest to enter. He shouts that Mom will live forever. She stands under an oak tree with her mouth open, her lips highlighted in red crystals. His eyes rocket into clouds raining sparks. His right foot slides out from beneath him. Heel on sky, his left leg upright, he floats across the sky with the village and beach and forest below.

Then the prison gets real quiet. The PA announces lights out. A voice from the upper level, might be Jeremy, screams to be taken back to the village where things are simple and quiet, people love each other there, and someone says *People might love you there but here you're just annoying.*

Pants McDonovan jumps into bed and is soon asleep and back on the beach. Mine workers dressed in mud wearing clear masks ask if he wants to die and he answers *I'm ready.* Harvak runs at his side. He says to him *No illness that's my fault will take Mom away, come on, we're breaking out of here.* The prison is quiet with only the night-shift steps of guards as Mom opens a door in the oak tree.

35

The heat wave continues. The elderly don't wear their traditional robes anymore. Few possess air conditioners donated by the city charity group, Mob of Mary's, who make bi-monthly runs into the village with clothing and canned meat. Those who do have Relief Gatherings where people take five minute turns in an air conditioned room where they smile in splayed out naked forms across a marble slab. At night they pray to their crystal collections for snow. Green crystals melt in direct sunlight. The leader of Brothers Feast, Z., finger-painted the green across his forehead in three bug-smeared lines. From the way he's dressed, the heat doesn't seem to bother him. The elders question his mental health.

Younger villagers who are against Brothers Feast, who have inherited land from the older generations, believe in selling to the city for reasons of safety. They believe the transfer of land will somehow spare their lives. The elderly have become conservative with their land, not wanting to give anything up. There have been secret discussions near The Bend with rogue mine workers willing to sell out and city politicians hungry to consume. The differences between the two cultures are absurdly obvious when a mine worker tells Sanders he has to get back to the mine to melt the yellow for the night's electricity. Another mine worker asks what each of their counts are and Sanders says, "We're good."

Dad says, the only one smiling, "Was the stove left on over night? Remy, see if the refrigerator is overheating."

Houseplants kept in shade and usually watered daily by Remy have wilted to cooked leaves of spinach because Remy is consumed with what is happening to Mom, not the heat, fuck the heat. But she knows it's getting worse. The forks and spoons on the kitchen table burn to the touch. Remy imagines the moon as a bucket of water she kicks over, cooling the sun below. Parts of her body that never sweat like the margins of her lips, her ears, her nail beds, are now continuously covered in sweat. The day's heat runs into the following day and the following day after that with no break, only a build-up, a layering of more. She sits at the kitchen table eating another meal prepared by Dad, taps her knee ten times while watching Mom doing nothing but staring into whatever she sees in the blank space before her. Remy thinks she hears a dog barking inside the house. She thinks about touching Mom. She worries about Dad, his decision making.

In direct correlation to Mom, Dad has lost several crystals. When he jokes in his passive-aggressive way *See if the refrigerator is overheating* Remy can't look at his awkward smirk, his do-nothing ways with Mom sitting skeletal. Dad's strategy is to let time make all decisions, but with Mom rapidly losing her count, he wonders if he's wrong, wonders deep down if doing nothing will just end in a faster zero. But he still believes in time and nature and tradition. How Remy sees the world is something three dimensional and lit up, where Dad sees an endless and flat blackness.

Mom's room is the coolest in the house. Disease moves faster in heat. She has a red box with a green felt top. Inside, a black crystal given to her by her son. He never explained its use and Mom keeps it a secret from Dad and Remy. Her son, not the myth of Royal Bob, is the only person to ever find the black crystals. Some of the desperate elderly, closing down, believe in what he and The Sky Father Gang were trying to accomplish but they've never seen something like a black crystal. Mom walks into her room.

She plays a game when the sun reaches a special height in the sky. She sits down. The sun splits the window in the shape of a triangle and from the doorway her spine is visible through her nightgown. Her body aches with no sleep nights because not only is her count well below fifty, Mom basically a cat, but the number is falling incredibly fast now and she can feel it leaving her body. The game helps.

From the box she takes out the black crystal and dips it into the sunlight. The triangle warps and skinny lines of light reflect off the crystal. Mom tilts her hand until a hologram of another black crystal appears above the one she holds.

During her best games she produces eight crystal holograms attached to the black crystal she holds by eight beams of light. The highest touches the ceiling, the lowest flickers near her ear, and once, she moved her head until half the crystal disappeared into her hair.

Last week she stretched her fingers into positions that burned her joints. Her heart skipped a beat. The illness scratched her skin, ran the slopes of her body. She stopped the game when she heard Remy and Dad arguing about Twinning.

Today she plays the game perfectly. She dominates the sun. Twin horses float above her hand. She smiles because horses are new. She's 5'4 in height, her gown drags through hallways, but she feels like a giant creating holograms from the black crystal she holds and now, horses. Their bodies are a blue-black shine and they stomp their hooves and radiate six ribs of light across the room. For a moment, her life is a delirious and beautiful dream, something worth extending.

When she drops the black crystal from exhaustion, feeling

sick, the floor seems to sink into the room below where Dad and Remy are looking up.

34

The baby slept in the shade of the red pencil Remy had used and the drawing took up most of the wall.

"That's new," Dad said and pointed at the drawing.

"Bored of blue and yellow so I drew a red, no big deal. Dad, what's Twinning?"

"You drew a baby."

"Just felt like it."

"Does it mean anything?"

"Not really."

When Dad walked into the room days before, Harvak was on a table under a blue sheet with a wreath of hair balanced on top. Walking from the room Dad had a terrible feeling, something like anger, that became sour inside him when he convinced himself not to process what he was feeling. Since he was a boy he always managed his feelings this way because it felt safer to live this way. It hurt to take the feelings, drag them up and through his body, twist and mold them into words that he had to force from his mouth. Besides, having those words interpreted by another person was dangerous. Language distorts emotions. What he did, even as a little boy, for example, standing in a dark room full of strange adults, was erase the emotions before they could exit him in words. He told Remy, without looking at her, that Twinning didn't exist. A hard and simple no.

"You sure?"

He mentioned those who cut themselves with crystals. They believed in ascending count, and in a stunt similar to the things Brothers Feast does, marched into the city only to be imprisoned. They preached about Twinning and carried banners that read WE WILL BE REMEMBERED AND LIVE FOREVER. Dad didn't mention his son participating because denial is holy. He stopped talking and stared blankly ahead, fighting the flickering images of his son walking toward the city, away from him, the sun nothing but a pinprick in the blue.

"Did it work?" Remy asked bouncing on the bed. "They add?"

He forced himself to look at her. "They are in jail. The point is, sorry, your hood is falling down and I can't see your eyes. There, better. What I'm trying to say is, what is it I'm saying, yes, they went crazy with those crystals they found, trying to do what you're talking about. Extending a life, come on now, you're just a person and your life is special because of that."

"Black crystal moves your insides," said Remy. "Kids in my school say it changes your blood, and they're still buried underground. What do you have to say about that?"

"I wouldn't listen because who knows who their parents are. Adults get weirder and weirder as they get older. Everyone has their opinions but you're mine, you listen to me."

"Tell me again about the Gang," she said, feeling embarrassed. "I like when you tell me."

"Okay, I can do that."

Remy knew the story about The Sky Father Gang to near memory but wanted to hear Dad talk, she wanted his words, his soft words, in the air surrounding her.

They were seven kids who dressed in identical red robes with black hoods and black belts. What they believed in was different from Brothers Feast who waste their time with stunts (the village is so accustomed to them that their last stunt, pretending to dig up the crystal mine road with comically large cardboard shovels while dressed as city residents in navy blue suits donated by Mob of Mary's, everyone ignored). Remy remembered Brother being in The Sky Father Gang and she knew where he was now, prison. She remembered him with a duffel bag full of crystals, ready to leave forever, and she remembered how long his hair had grown down his back, and she remembered how distant he was to her, to everyone, to everything. It wasn't him anymore.

Mom went into the bathroom and closed the door.

The Sky Father Gang wanted to live longer. They founded their belief based on certain blue and yellow crystals Twinning. These crystals shared a similar lattice structure and grew together, intertwined. If Twinning existed outside the body, why not in? Why couldn't you double what you already had? These were the questions they had asked, were forgotten about with their imprisonment, and the questions Remy now resurrected and Dad tried to repeal.

She leaned into his words.

Experimenting with black crystal is what drove The Sky Father Gang into the city, wide-eyed and tongue-out. Boys and girls in undone robes showing crystal laced underwear screwed and bled in city streets. Brother didn't wear any underwear, only robe. They took turns inserting crystals inside each other's holes and created new openings in their stomachs, chests, and thighs. People took pictures on phones and uploaded them to websites. The city charged the village to remove the crystals, to repair the bruised bones and missing skin at a place called a hospital. Rumors in the village said The Sky Father Gang were close to finding a solution to increasing count. Brother wanted Mom to live forever. A news report showed them jumping in the courtroom, skeletal-lunging faces spitting on a pale-faced judge with thinning red hair. Cameras followed. The Sky Father Gang kicked a table over and laughed with their heads tilted back. Veins webbed their bodies. They tackled a guard, everyone falling to the floor in a crashing wave, and the Gang spun their bodies by kicking their feet against the floor. Brother howled in a fish-flop directly on top of the guard. Brother was the loudest. Brother was raw. Remy believed in what he was trying to accomplish. Why not try if that's all there is to do.

Dad loosened the fur collar of his robe. He told Remy it was too hot to be wearing these but she insisted he talk more and he agreed, wanting, needing, to connect with his daughter who on some mornings he didn't recognize. Sometimes, when she entered a room, the size of her startled him, as if a stranger had entered the house, and he'd jump in his chair and wonder where the biggest knife in the kitchen was.

In the bathroom, the porcelain clink of the toilet bowl raised by Mom.

"What about eating them?" Remy asked.

"Tried that. Very sick."

"Was it red? Have you ever seen a black crystal? Kids at school say no one has seen one after The Sky Father Gang. Other kids say black crystals never existed at all, that it's only a story made up by people with sad brains. The older you get the more you believe in it, kind of like what you said before about adults getting weirder. If I found one I'd probably try it. Yeah, I would. I heard people believe – "

"Hey, why are you thinking this?"

"Because," said Remy, "I want to prepare myself so I don't suffer like Harvak. I don't want to feel pain. People remember your suffering and the last memory they have of you is your face and I don't want mine to be hurting. I want to help Mom."

"You shouldn't spend your life worrying about dying."

"Unavoidable."

"Why?"

"To not think *hm* wonder what's my count, while you're alive? I don't think you can ignore the thoughts of zero. It's scary to be alive. Sometimes, if I close my eyes and clear my head and just concentrate, like just really concentrate on what it would be like to be empty, to not have to live, to not get out of bed, my entire body goes into a kind of shock. It knows. I can feel what it will be like."

"City people don't think that. They may not agree with us, but they just live their lives, I think. They just keep expanding and moving and, well, I don't think they have time to think. Maybe it's better."

"I bet they don't believe it until they are about to die and start apologizing on their death bed. I saw a fat woman jogging The Bend and I barked at her. I'm sorry, but I did it." Remy laughed the same child laugh she's had since having a hundred inside and for a quick moment, like a finger poke between his ribs, it breaks him.

"Don't be scared by what you can't control."

He looked around the room. His daughter was outgrowing the space he once proudly provided. He should have built the room larger, with a deeper closet for her games, clothes, art supplies taken from Mob of Mary's, books on count, dozens of blue and yellow pillows, a poster of the sun.

"Must be hard knowing there isn't a way to help her. You just watch. Maybe Brother never did find a black crystal because if he did he would have given it to Mom and she wouldn't be sick. There's a kid in my school named John who says they were just dark red all along. You know what, I'll find the solution so we'll all live longer. I'll do it."

"What did you get on your spelling test?"

Mom vomited red slush, lost another crystal, and dabbed her mouth with the spitting cloth. The bathroom tiles on her palms were comforting. She stretched out and lay on the floor in front of the toilet, face turned to the side and smushed against the cool tiles. She thought about horses.

"Haven't gotten it back. I know why they want to move in. Because we're different. Because they want to see, and then they want to take, what they don't understand. We're living a life they think is silly. Sometimes I feel like everything is pushing inward. You said I'll always have one crystal inside me as long as Mom's alive."

He wanted to say more and be comfortable inside the words to connect them. He couldn't. His body carried him from the room. His body protected him. The imaginary conversation hurt too much. He stood in the doorway.

"She okay?"

"I'll check."

"Will this heat wave ever end?"

The universe breaths billions of worlds. The earth is tiny, but possesses crystals the sun is drawn to. The universe allows the sun to get closer, to create a heat wave across the city and the village, to become pulled by what is buried under the earth's crust. This is another type of game.

33

Brother screams for Remy. With an arm three times longer than normal length he reaches through the circular door. His hand is several inches short from touching Remy who is crystallized in yellow light. He tries to extend his arm but the several inches short begin working backward until he's being pulled over an ocean, fingertips spraying water, body dissected by a lighthouse. Somewhere near, Harvak is barking.

A cloud in the shape of a mouth leans over the bed and chomps away at the crystals in severe animal angles. Cloud-teeth splinter and fly like spit fingernails. The mouth destroys itself into a million clouds. Remy presses two yellow crystals to her ears, tosses and turns and screams *Mom can't die because Mom is Mom, Mom can't die because Mom is a god,* tosses and turns, *Mom can't die because Mom is a dog, Mom can't die because a dog is a god,* tosses and turns, *Mom can't die because Mom is my Mom and my Mom is forever,* tosses and turns until blue slush sprays from her mouth in a bridge to the ceiling. When she sneezes, the yellow crystal dust inside her nose becomes pollen-colored mist and she is pulled up and through the mist, through the circular door, and from the bed. Crystals fall from her feet like a gown. The bridge crumbles to salt, then rain. Animal paws press down on her and she hears herself breathing in the otherwise silence of the room.

Remy opens her eyes, shakes the strange dream away, and

pets a barking dog at her side. It's young, shorthaired, brown, with floppy ears that she pinches and rubs. One eye is yellow, the other black. She's not sure where the dog came from, but she can hear Dad running through the house slamming doors. She hides the dog in her closet and listens to his nails scratch the door.

"Shhhhhhhhhhh," she says to the closet.

The dog lets out a small yelp.

"Shhhh, be quiet."

When Dad comes in he's covered in sweat and his face is roasted. He doesn't say anything, looks mad at first, then takes a deep breath that relaxes his jaw and he sits down on the bed the way all Dads do. But there's a weakness to his posture that wasn't there before. His left hand is stained yellow. Every home is using more YCL because of the heat wave and there's been talk amongst elders of stockpiling yellow. Dad believes that the value of yellow will rise until it's equal to red but no one else believes him. In his closet he has three denim jackets, twelve pockets total, all stuffed with yellow crystals.

"Remy?"

"That was the weirdest dream ever. It was like, more than a dream. Like I was sick or something. My foot hurts. I've been running in the mine and, I don't know, it was more."

"I'm not angry," he says looking around the room, "just tell me."

"What?"

"Remy, come on now."

"Seriously, whaaaaaaaat."

"You know."

"I don't."

The dog barks.

Dad leaps from the bed and in three steps reaches the closet and opens it. The dog jumps out and runs circles around his legs.

"I didn't do anything wrong. He just came into my room after my nap. On my test I got a C minus."

"We were going to try and hide him until your birthday. It was your Mother's idea."

In the presence of Dad, in the way the dog is revealed to her, Remy feels like she's done something wrong, feels guilty, and she's not sure why, other than this is how the family operates. He doesn't acknowledge hearing her test score and she doesn't wait for it to register.

"Dad," she says. "Can I ask you a question?"

"Sure."

"Anything?"

"Yeah."

"Why did you hurt Adam?"

"Because."

"Dad?"

"Anything."

"Are you dying because Mom is dying?"

"What kind of question is that?"

She sits up. The dog jumps into her bed and licks her face. The yellow eye is dull and the black is shining. His gums look black and pink and chewed up.

"Last night I saw Mom crawling across the floor."

"He likes you. She's resting and everything's fine."

"You said I could ask anything."

"And you did."

"What do you name a dog after your first dog dies?"

32

All prison cells are decorated with the exception of Jackson's Hole which is located behind the laundry room and has no lights, no running water, is four feet by four feet, and smells like chemical lavender. Imagination by the inhabitant is encouraged. The administration is proud to promote this fact to curious city residents who skim glossy magazines and blogs for prison gossip. Reports of creativity make the inmates more human to workers in cubicles who spend their days living in screens. When they read about a prisoner painting a mural of skeletons wrapped in roses on a wall in the courtyard where the inmates exercise, it's not with fear, but relief and an odd sense of comfort and admiration.

Guards interact with the inmates in a friendly but reserved manner. Fights are occasional. By the low night level noise it seems everyone sleeps well. The administration is also proud of this detail and reports often to the press how calm the prison can be because a calm prison makes the inmates seem less capable of the terrible acts they are guilty of. For example, there is a man named DeWeese, housed on the upper level, who is Grade A. DeWeese is polite, rarely speaks, and volunteers shelving history books in the library. He gives blood every Monday, both drunk-tattooed arms exposed, his face a big warm smile blasting the nurse. Multiple pool owners watched from inside their homes as DeWeese performed what he is guilty of: drowning squirrels in paint buckets.

Pants McDonovan lives on lower level east, and from his cell bars sees the upper level where more than fifty villagers are mixed in with hundreds of city prisoners. Many of them wandered into the city because they were attracted by streetlamps, big buildings, festive music, a new way of life, a way to start over, but they couldn't adjust. They slept nude on street corners, dipped their toes into crosswalks, pawned crystals in trash-lined bricked alleys without permits. An elderly man with long gray hair wearing blue shorts prayed for ten hours to a storefront of televisions on please-stand-by. At night he smashed out the glass and threw the televisions into the streets, the colored bars on the screen cracking to distant lines the color of iron. How many villagers are in the prison isn't widely known, especially not to Pants who occasionally recognizes a depressed face hovering over macaroni salad during cafeteria hours, but he's never tried to keep track. The village knows about their people being imprisoned. Makes them suspicious about the city's intent.

New inmates are stuffed inside a briefing zone on the upper level covered with blue mesh before being moved into their cells. Often, they are heckled from the lower levels by everyone except Pants who only watches, feeling awful about seeing men being placed in here, sometimes unconsciously tapping his thumb and pointer-finger together in sets of ten.

Upper level inmates complain about the temperature. In the current heat wave sleeping is pretty much impossible and the administration has poorly addressed the problem by installing cooling vents to offset what is a serious design flaw. Prisoners throw cups, food trays, books, spoons, their shoes, their teeth, whatever will learn to fly, at a window they hope will one day break. The lower levels are cool, dry, a design-flaw-mystery, which agrees with Pants who consumes so much black crystal his body temperature runs ten degrees above average. Because the administration considers him *an agreeable and mild-mannered inmate who possesses a crystal that the guards have taken a liking to (Grade A)* he's in charge of laundry duties three days a week and allowed an extra shower with the heat turned up to a skin-reddening temperature.

Your cell is a reflection of your inner self.

McDonovan spent more time decorating his cell than all currently housed inmates combined. His mattress is cradled inside a hull of plastic branches. The headboard becomes an octopus when he's on black crystal, and the ceiling a forever green that welcomes him in moans. He enters it. He peels back layers of forest as the ceiling breaths and he goes inside, splitting ferns. But as soon as he enters, he's back on the bed. Drawings of black crystals on white paper hang on the walls all signed *Love, Remy.* The cement floor is the color of the dirt in the crystal mine – painted in an unusual, but allowed by the administration, "Universal Black." White lights caged-in on the ceiling polish the floor with glare. A toilet is in one corner, a square sink adjacent extends from the wall, and a two-foot-deep closet without a door containing clothes and a white box completes the living quarters, the *reflection.*

A window allows Pants to view the ugly blocks of the city and a curved road called The Bend where people the size of fleas sweat and jog. Below The Bend, the cliff leading to the village.

You have done wrong, but you are an individual with choices and we allow you to be yourself here. You are an individual constantly becoming a better individual.

Tonight he studies his reflection in the window. If he concentrates hard enough he floats through his head and home, into what is childhood-him playing spit-tag with Remy, jumping on his bike as motorcycle, finger-shooting Remy as he pedals away in a dust cloud with Remy running, falling several times, crying, laughing, spitting on herself, Mom watching, standing with her arms crossed and clutching at her throat a necklace of ten yellow crystals. After the childhood him smokes into the sun, the bike turning to blue gas beneath him, everything becoming a runny liquid hiss over the ground, he's brought back into his cell and wonders when Mom will write next, how is she feeling, how many does she have left.

He looks forward to her letters. Remy's been asking about count, his involvement in The Sky Father Gang, if a black crystal exists or not, does touching your body in sets of ten do anything or does it just feel good. He tells Mom the only black left is the one in her possession. His gift to her when he was scared and didn't know what it was. When he first found the black crystals during the endless rainstorm he made sure to hide them from everyone, even himself, because he didn't believe what he held. The rumors of it spread. *People just need something to believe in.* It turned out he was no different. He wanted Mom to live forever so he gave it to her.

He opens his mouth and stabs a sliver of black crystal inside his cheek. In the window a blue honeycomb-hexagon frames his mouth, eyes, every joint, tooth, fissure, nerve, and canal. The human skull stripped to bone is smiling. A fire rises from his stomach and when he coughs is blown across his chest. Ears hurt. Throat constricts. Hair echoes Mother. He stands looking at his head, his big ugly head that is even bigger today on his narrowing, via the black crystal, shoulders. When he stomps his feet the boom rattles his teeth. He grins and sees not the reality of the blood in his mouth but a thousand red crystals. Then, he sees something new. Mom's patting a cut on his knee with his own shirt, the injury from falling off his bike, his motorcycle, after the game of spit-tag with Remy. She's discussing the concept of pain. *It's when the crystals inside your body go out.* She explains by touching the cut with a press of the shirt. *They are trying to turn back on, that's why it hurts.* She stops pressing. *Trust me, they'll come back on, here.* She pushes the shirt deep into the cut and he wants to be strong for her so he holds back tears and grins while grabbing fistfuls of grass. *Your body is getting brighter, I see it.* He smiles and a cry escapes. She presses again, this time lighter, and he shuts his eyes. *You're at a hundred again.*

When a guard passes his cell McDonovan reaches into his pocket and drops a mini plastic bag filled with black dust through the bars. The guard says, "Thank ya, business man Pants," and skips off to tell four more guards that the bags are ready.

Back in the reflection he tilts his head to the left and the hexagon doesn't follow. He moves more, then a little more, and then a little more, until he's standing to the side of the window, slightly below, crouching. He craves it but knows it's not true — the black crystal increasing his count. When he reaches up and places his palm on the hexagon it morphs to fit the twenty-seven bones in his hand. Pants laughs, his head turtling into his shoulders. Inmates are yelling from above.

Tony throws a sharpened spoon and it bounces off the window. Everyone goes *AHHHHHHHNOOOOOOOOOOO.* The noise snaps McDonovan to the right. The hexagon is gone. The prison gets quiet. Pete, from the upper level says *Next time instead of a spoon use, like, your own body or some shit* and he realizes that doesn't make any sense at all so he follows up with a vague *just use a really sharp spoon, okay.* The heat wave is killing them with sleep deprivation. They can't think straight. Pete rubs his face with both hands and goes dizzy. Someone coughs and Pants turns again. His head feels like a microwave heating spoons. Four guards stand in a row with their right arms extended through his cell bars, hands open.

31

It's time for a crystal mine search.

They find yellow nuggets and blue shale. The sun fell hours ago but left its heat pinned like a dress in the sky and everyone moves slow beneath it. Remy wears dirty red shorts and her blond hair hangs over the front of her shoulders. Her dog, whom she calls Dog Man because she can't settle on a name – seems impossible to move on from Harvak – digs up a green crystal and she grabs it and slides it into her pocket.

"Keep looking. We'll find it. Keep going, Dog Man."

Brothers Feast walk past discussing a jailbreak in reverse. A hairless man slows and smirks at Remy as the others walk ahead shoving each other and laughing on the road out. The man smells like dead dogs and Remy instinctively begins tapping her finger on her thigh. Moonlight filtered through trees forms a birdcage around his head. Remy throws dirt into the air and he ducks, not sure where it will land until it's heard raining on a truck's hood and he stands back up with a jump.

He says, "Freak-o," and walks backward three steps before turning and catching up to the group, tripping once and falling to his knees before picking himself up and running again even though he's hurt and badly limping.

"Smell you later," she says, remembering the saying from a city show she once heard from the family radio while sitting in

Brother's lap. He had new hair on his arms and she had no idea what the phrase meant but she loved it and wrote the words several dozen times in her school notebook around and inside of previous drawings of crystals.

Remy tells Dog Man that if she can increase her count she will possess the power to reverse Mothers. She pictures Mom gathering crystals by the valley-full with flowered fingers, light radiating in tunnels from her mouth and eyes, green looping inside her body from throat to stomach in an endless U. A tunnel of light from her left eye connects to Brother and guides him across a bridge built from prison to her. Just for her. Brother comes back to the house and into a seated position with Remy in his lap pulling his hairy arms over the front of her body. The radio shouting cartoons. The family at full count forever. Mom says, making eye contact with Remy inside the dream, cartoons blaring rain and cars and speech bubbles *We have one person to thank and it's Remy!*

"Come on, dig more."

He looks up at her before churning the ground with alternating paws, nose down.

"I know they exist."

Yesterday Mom spent the afternoon in her room. She dropped something heavy on the floor that moved the house. Inside the drawing on the wall of the red crystal, the baby moved, and suddenly, Remy hated the drawing and wanted it gone. Dad was with her, and they both looked up before looking at each other, no idea what causes a thudding sound like that – dense, sharp, centered. Remy asked for paint. Later, Dad walked out of the room and ran to the bathroom to see if Mom was okay. Remy waited and waited, nothing to do with her fingers but tap her knees until falling asleep, only to be told when she woke from the weirdest dream ever, a new dog on her lap, that yes, Mom was fine, nothing to worry about.

But she took forever to descend the stairs that night for

dinner which was pork chops seared gold with garlic potatoes prepared by Dad who was wearing the same stained clothes. When Remy asked what was wrong he spoke with food mashed in his mouth, said she was sick, an illness, old age, *How about we don't talk about it right now, we went over this before, okay? Play with your* *new dog.* Several times during dinner Mom was given the spitting cloth for the red drizzling her chin and throat. Her face looked scared, almost childish, and pained in a way that made Remy tell herself she would do anything to help, even sacrifice herself.

A loud bang and Remy says, "Buildings coming from the city? Dig around more, hurry."

Dog Man doesn't look up, his nose buried inside a cone of dirt.

Remy has had nights where she can't sleep, thinking about her parents, Brother, the family pulled like puppets away from each other, strings severed by stars. Disease cuts all. Remy wonders when she too will catch an illness and rush toward zero. She wonders what it feels like to have nothing inside. What will she see in those final seconds? Will there be colors?

"Last try."

Something is happening in the city: sky-stretched screams, ambulance howls, rising smoke, breaking glass. The Brothers leave the mine by way of the dirt road and run to watch. The moon weakens from clouds. In a final attempt to find a black crystal Remy picks a random spot on the ground and makes a hole by kicking her heel downward. Dog Man barks. Nothing. Not even yellow. Remy hears the noises too, sees the trails of smoke above, wonders what it could be.

They run up the road and out of the mine and watch the fire in the city. Night-framed bodies leap from a burning building before ladders can fall against the roof. The moon pulls flames from the windows in ribbons of yellow and red. Six arcs of water extend from flashing lights positioned below. At this distance, in this moonlight, when a helicopter turns and slants itself when pouring dirt from above and onto the burning building the helicopter disappears and what Remy sees is a slit in the sky spewing dirt. She looks and wonders where the hospital is. Dog Man moans.

"It's okay," she says, holding him in her arms, his nose wet and covered in dirt. "That's city fire."

"You'll let me die like Harvak."

"I won't," says Remy.

"I'm not really talking," says Dog Man. "I eat my own shit."

"Will Mom die?"

A large temple-shaped flame spurts skyward from the roof and more people scream.

"That is *exactly* what will happen."

"Then what's the point?"

Trucks driving toward the fire drown buildings in flashing lights. Curious faces hang from apartment windows. Someone drops their phone ten stories and shouts, "My phone!"

Dog Man says, "They consume because they want to live forever."

"I don't know what that means."

The chopping of the helicopter narrows to a distant and silent dot.

"I sleep under your bed and puke there. There's an entire floor of puke and you don't know about it."

"Why are you telling me that?"

He laugh-barks. "A lake of puke."

"Stop it."

"Puke ocean."

"Let's go."

"Puke city."

"Come on."

"Puke kingdom."

"We're going now."

"You know what you are?"

"What?"

"The princess of castle puke."

They run home with the smoke and clouds and heat a union above, following.

Remy wakes in her bed. She sneezes black gunk into her palm and wipes her hand on the flower-print bedspread. When she stands, she steps on her sleeping dog and immediately jumps to the side, raising her foot.

"Sorry," she says.

"..."

"Hey, said I was sorry."

Dog Man sits up, head angled.

"I'm not looking under the bed."

"..."

"How is Mom?"

"..."

After washing her hands in the bathroom Remy walks downstairs. Smell of bacon. She trips on a bucket of YCL placed on the floor just around the corner to the kitchen entrance. Some of it sloshes out and spills on the floor and Dad yells because they need every drop. Remy cleans the spill up with a wet cloth from the sink and Dad watches her every move.

Dad attempts to get Mom to eat a sliced apple with honey. She eats with hesitation, little interest, her mouth caged with saliva. Her eyes say she wants the bacon on the stove, Remy sees this, but Dad doesn't notice. He holds the apple to her lips. Dad prepares meal after meal to show he cares. He spends countless hours cooking only to rush through eating and then moving on to the next meal. He thinks time spent together at the table is important, family time, a duty and obligation that must be filled, but you wouldn't guess it by watching his rushed movements that he cared, never asking what they would actually like to eat.

Sunlight sprays the kitchen window and everything from the

wet cloth towels in the sink to the legs of the wooden chairs to the YCL in the bucket gets hotter.

"I figured out his name," says Remy.

"Uh-huh," says Mom. She smiles. She asks if Remy wants some apple. There's honey near the breadbox. Again, she eyes the bacon.

"Hundred."

"Come on now," says Dad, still looking at Mom. He opens his mouth so Mom opens her mouth. It doesn't work. Then his voice gets sharper: "Why'd you pick such a terrible name?"

"It means he's full. A living creature who will never lose his count. Like a person. Hundred."

Dad bites his bottom lip. "It means," he says and then stops, composes himself. "It means," he says, this time even softer, "that every time you look at him you will think about your count."

"But," says Remy.

"Change it."

"I think," says Mom, "it's a beautiful name."

Her voice is strong.

"It's death obsessed," says Dad. "It's not a name. It's not a name a little girl gives her pet."

Mom stares at Dad and something shifts inside him because here is something Mom wants for her daughter, she doesn't ask for much, and he knows it. Remy grabs the bacon.

"You can name your dog whatever you want. Hundred is perfect. I love it," Mom says. "Hundred! Hundred! Hundred! Is beautiful! Beautiful! Beautiful! Hundred! Hundred! Hundred! Is beautiful! Beautiful! Beautiful!"

Remy starts singing along with Mom.

Hundred comes running so fast into the kitchen that he sweeps the length of the floor with his body.

30

She called him Dog Man. She wore red shorts and dug in the dirt for crystals. When she threw dirt at Bobby T.'s face he crouched in the darkness and rocks clanged off truck metal.

Arnold said, "Hurry up, Bobby T.," so he did, he ran.

In the distance a building burned. Z. said the girl was Remy. Her Brother was the founder of The Sky Father Gang. Remy acting like a dog was normal, that when she stands she looks like any teenager. Her family has hellish problems so it's her way of getting things out of her, don't call her a freak-o. Bobby T. made an *Ahhhhhh* sound while nodding emphatically and said, "That makes sense," though he wasn't sure it did.

Viewing the building illuminated with fire they applauded.

Then they walked to their favorite spot to admire the prison. They kicked wind-blown garbage at the holes in the fence. The night sky was starless and smoky with a full moon. Everything felt crushable, even the trees. Z. had a feeling he couldn't define that rattled him, made his heart hurt. He wanted to be more than a person. He wanted to live through people's memories and through history, something his grandfather once told him, to pass along stories and myths (some of which he wrote), that's how you live forever, become part of another's reality after you're gone. This talk has never left Z., the words coming just before his grandfather went to zero, his parents screaming to not watch, leave the room, stop standing in the corner like that. Z. has the idea of a colossal performance burning into the minds of thousands, his name inked in books and scatter-dropped into computers.

The Brothers, about a dozen of them, ran until they leaned their chests into the fence and pressed their faces against the metal wire that left hexagons on their skin. Bobby T. played the song of the dirt and rocks clanging off the truck in his head and moved into a warm spot of good while the prison shimmered like a heaven.

Z. fantasized about the jailbreak in reverse and tried to untie the knot of what it was. All the images were murky, people running in and out of the prison without reason. Bobby T. faced him, the prison now at his back. Mouth twisted, Z. was thinking it out, pacing like a starved cat, mind on overdrive, mouth mumbling at high speed. He said they had to do more than protests. He stopped and jumped forward, leering at Bobby T., and said it involved breaking out The Sky Father Gang. His hand was a sleeping spider on Bobby T.'s shoulder and Bobby T. looked scared to move. "A j-j-j-jailbreak in reverse," Z. said and stepped away. "A jail... break... in... r-r-r-reverse?" He scratched his head. "Breaking out of a prison, but twisted, reversed, inmates entering a prison in exchange for inmates already inside. Or maybe it's... who knows what it is because I'm the o-o-o-one who can d-d-d-define it."

"We'll do it," Bobby T. said, not knowing what he meant exactly but feeling uncomfortable with Z. and thinking he had to say something, anything, to break the strangeness. He looked at Ricky and shrugged and Ricky shrugged back.

"I'll do it all right," mumbled Z. more to himself than to Bobby T.

Z. wore a green robe in the old style. The collar and wrists were white and fur lined. His feet were covered in dirty white sneakers with fat tongues. Extreme heat didn't bother him. He randomly shouted, "This heat wave is a joke!" The robe belonged to his grandfather and held memory and magic. His eyes were the color of truck exhaust. His stutter came and went, but the closer he got to defining the jailbreak in reverse, the less it appeared. He would erase it. He would become smooth and living forever in people's memories. When he spoke, the Brothers believed and followed every word, sentence, idea, believing that Z. was powerful and special and would eventually change their lives too.

"Question," Z. said. "Your attention, please."

They turned their backs on the prison, joined Bobby T., and leaned into the slight give of the fence. Bobby T. tongue-clicked rock noises and stopped when Z. gave him a real serious look.

Arnold said, "Let's do this thing," to which Z. rolled his eyes and allowed a moment of shame. "Sorry," said Arnold.

In the breeze Z.'s green robe fluttered open. He wore a white t-shirt and had a belly that he quickly covered up. "How many of you are w-w-w-willing to go into the prison with me?"

Everyone raised their hands and their upper backs fell into the give of the fence.

"That's what I thought," he said, and again began mumbling the phrase "jailbreak in reverse" while pacing back and forth as the Brothers breathed in nothing but the hot air of their doomed land.

"Let's do this thing," repeated Arnold, and this time, Z. nodded and pointed with both hands at the prison and wouldn't stop nodding until Ricky asked if he was okay.

29

On a typical morning he spends three hours in the laundry room, which is fifteen degrees warmer than the second-floor cells. The laundry room is a miniature warehouse of cleaning in the color gray. Hot air hangs like a curtain on a movable track. Metal tables edge-lined with machine-drilled dimples hold clothing pressed in stacks. Washers and dryers built into ten towers shake in front of windows covered in blue X wire. The sun creates bars of light through the steam and the outline of McDonovan's body is visible while he irons a heap of shirts.

He silences his ears with toilet paper. In the afternoon part-time workers from Open Skies Cleaning Service arrive and finish whatever he didn't get to. Having someone the administration can trust, like Pants, is cheap, allows them to pay less to Open Skies, and he does an exceptional job (Grade A, extra shower time, full heat), resulting in his nickname which makes him feel belittled, like when Dad called him "tiny man." Not "little man" like some fathers lovingly call their sons, but "tiny man" in a tone that cut. The way he runs a crease from the thigh to kneecap before dropping to the ankle the guards can't figure out. When Pants tells them he was an artist of sorts, in Sky Father, they nod, not understanding what participation in Sky Father has to do with working an iron like a seamstress. He says when he was a boy his parents made him clean and iron his underwear until they looked new, the fabric thin and stretched, because it was part of a punishment, maybe that's where he gets his talent from. The guards smile, don't respond or ask about the punishment, and they walk away, which makes Pants feel worse, makes him feel like "tiny man."

After the laundry shift, a guard, one of the few who don't use, escorts him back to his cell where the weekly letters sit on his bed. The guard discusses the heat wave and the politicians debating whether to move in to the village or not.

"When the lord speaks his decision will echo through the politicians, like Sanders," says the guard who sports a gold cross on a gold necklace. "The village doesn't believe in a god and that's what's wrong. You believe in rocks."

"The yellow ones are power," says Pants. "You melt them into YCL. It's important. Please stop talking. Thank you."

"God wants civilized people to move into the village, which is godless. You see what I'm saying? Us moving in is a good thing for you people. We trust Sanders. It's an opportunity to become educated in the ways of god and learn what actual medicine is. It's impossible for you people to keep living the way you do as time moves forward."

Pants says that the city gets what the city wants because of chaos, not god. He says they don't want what they have to offer because the village has always been fine without the city. He again tells the guard to please stop talking, thank you.

The guard sneers, touches his cross. He's heard the rumors before about the city nearing, buildings randomly sprouting up. The guard prays nightly. He doesn't necessarily believe that a city can grow on its own accord, something alive and wanting more. What he believes in is god doing all things right, for him.

"We'll see," says the guard, but Pants is already not listening, thinking about Mom and home and the letters waiting to be opened in his cell.

Correspondence with Mom concerns crystals. She describes in pencil drawn diagrams what the holograms look like that extend from the black crystal he gave her. *The last attempt,* she writes, *two black horses appeared. Twins. I call this Horses Hologram. Do you know this? I'm not crazy. Don't tell me that.* If he writes back asking if she's eating black crystal, she never answers. He knows nothing about horses. He doesn't think his Mom, whom he loves deeply and painfully, is in the slightest, crazy. He only wants to help her, but questions if his need to help is a way to lessen his own guilt because of what happened to her, and now, her sickness. Not because he's a good person. He ignores this question as quickly as it arrived.

His letters discuss the effects of black crystal and how the guards are hooked. *They believe in immortality under a universe that will silence them.* What he has will run out. He's convinced the guards that it increases longevity. They are good to him because he controls it. They don't steal it from him because they don't fully understand what the black crystal is besides village voodoo and aren't sure they want the responsibility of its possibilities, so they keep this game going with Pants and it's working out just fine. There is an understanding and a structure and that's what people need. Besides, what the hooked guards believe is this: the city will eventually take over and then they won't need Pants McDonovan ever again. They can study the mine and what the village lifestyle is like and finally be comfortable with what they now don't understand. They can bring the village into modern living with god, carpeted cubicles, televisions, dishwashers, tooth x-rays, nuggets, yoga, babysitters, meat, car washes, air conditioning with floral scents, jogging, speed dating, screens, cat-shaped headphones, keyboards, raw juice, leather interior coffins. The guards like getting high, feeling new and different, on the black crystal.

Black crystal just feels good he once wrote to Mom. *It makes the blood jump inside your body and nothing else. They are going to need more and I'm scared about that day coming too soon.*

He knows Mom is ill, she's mentioned it prior in letters, but he doesn't know how bad it's gotten, the layers of ache peeling up from her tiny screams, the rot expanding inside the tunnels inside her bones inside her body. If he could see her. If he could stand before her, he'd feel like a boy seeing her cry for the first time. How he watched hiding from the doorway his mother sob and shake under the bedsheets, and afterward, he realized while sitting on his bed and poking his stomach hard ten times, that she wasn't invincible like he had previously thought. He wanted her to live forever after he witnessed her and the men in the mine that night, shortly after seeing her cry. He could have done something, but he didn't. The men went back. *You could have done something* is a black mantra he repeats daily, an endless banner of *You could have done something* wrapping around his thoughts and getting tighter and tighter.

The cell door slams shut and distracts him from the memory. The guard tells him to believe in the power of god, the values of Sanders, and smooches his cross.

"Makes sense," says Pants with a goofy grin.

"Inside your body is a number of crystals."

"Not as ridiculous," says Pants mimicking the size of the guard's smile.

The guard wants to say something back, but decides to continue smirking, that's his answer back, and he walks from the cell, whistling, strutting, but feeling a little defeated.

In his last sent letter Pants described eating crystal. *Cold and sharp under my tongue before pressing it into my gums where it bleeds warm. Tastes pretty good.* He discussed the need to jog in place, the gelatinous sweat that rings his neck, the stench of damp crystal mine dirt evaporating from his skin, all his childhood memories burned in amber then stretched into the present positive to make the universe and his life seem less awful. He often wonders why, when he was a boy and he fought endlessly with Dad and in return Dad and Mom fought, did no one ask anyone else one obvious and critical question: are you happy? Once, while on black crystal, he had a dream where he stood behind Mom's legs as she stirred a cast iron pot rimmed in little green crystals on a stain-crusted stove. They were alone on a beach. The sand was cold. The delicate fabric of Mom's gown against her calves, his hands. He could taste salt blowing in the breeze. When he began to leave the dream, when he became aware of where he was, prison, the space between his cell's bars filled with waves.

I placed my tongue on a crystal I found in Remy's room, Mom writes. A yellow. I was scared to try the black. A metallic taste, lemony, and I pulled the crystal from my mouth and wiped it clean by dragging it over her mattress which I now feel guilty about. I didn't have the spitting cloth, but I wish I did because I vomited red and probably lost another, but you don't need to worry about me, I'm not crazy, don't you worry while you're in there. Do you remember when you and Remy played the tapping game?

On the second floor a fight breaks out between inmates and guards over the heat. A bottle shatters. The comically high-pitched Al LaValle, says, "Shake me but don't make me," as he's dragged to Jackson's Hole. Pants sees LaValle's limp body being wiped horizontally across the floor. Alarm bells ring and guards run. Some of the inmates are singing "Bye Bye Mr. Bad Guy," and LaValle, still on his back, still being dragged by the guards, is waving both hands to the rhythm.

He replies in his letter that he once wedged broken crystals under his toenails. Each nail on his right foot shined a different color: yellow was the pinkie toe, then blue, red, green, and black for the big toe. Throughout the day he scrunched his foot inside his boot and walked on the tops of his toes in ten-yard clips. People watched him walking odd from shack to shack and they shook their heads, pitied his strangeness. He sprinted across a busy street of mining trucks pumping their breaks and screamed and laughed, the feeling of coming alive through pain and crystals, before collapsing against a store wall and shaking, his feet ballooning with liquid as the candle maker himself told him to hurry along while poking him with a stick.

He opens the second letter on the bed. It's from Brothers Feast. He's received these letters before, a kind of fan mail from those following in the footsteps of The Sky Father Gang:

1) What's a jailbreak in reverse look like?
2) Would you like to leave the prison?

He grabs the white box from the closet and takes out the black crystal which is changing shape with use – in his palm it looks like two small intertwined pinecones. A passing guard who already appears maxed-out, eyes not looking like eyes, stops at his cell and stares. Pants picks off a crumb-edge that the guard takes. The guard smiles, places the crumb-edge under his tongue, and crab-walks away to the sound of ringing bells. Pants knows what's going on because he's seen it before: guards getting sky-high are messing with the alarms and jumping and laughing inside an office with bullet-proof glass. They are taking turns pressing their faces against the glass and blowing kisses until they pass out. The crab walking guard on his way back to the office is having too much fun, grinding his pelvis against the walls as he goes.

Pants sits back on the bed. With his front teeth he shaves off a layer of black dust from a flat side. He catches the dust on the top of his pointer finger, raises it to his nose, inhales, *poof.*

He writes back that a jailbreak in reverse would be criminals running into jail. Or no, a jailbreak in reverse would be criminals or people who belong in jail running into a jail and freeing everyone who doesn't belong in jail and the criminals staying in the jail. He rips the paper with hand speed. He's excited with the possibility of leaving as the thoughts, ideas, spin and tear at the *You could have done something* banner. He draws a square with arrows running in and bubble-lines running out. The arrows are labeled Brothers Feast and the bubble-lines The Sky Father Gang.

Answer to question two, this answer written with more control: *Yes and I will help you.* He's heard the prison looks real pretty from the outside, and who knows how much time is left before the city moves in. *Is it true the heat wave is only getting worse? From my window the sky looks faded from too much sun.* Beneath this he writes *Pretend to be inmates. One of you will play the role of a newbie transfer guard. Say it's for a transfer to a holding tank called Willows Bay. I'll leave with the others. Brothers Feast will remain inside the prison until they become legends in the village and then set free when the administration realizes what's happened. They won't, they can't, keep the foolish innocent. If there's a problem, just act insane. They never keep the crazies in here. If you can pull off breaking into the prison, you can later pull off breaking out of a psych ward. Just follow these guidelines…*

Pants McDonovan dances with black crystal inside him and the thought of leaving the prison. He closes his eyes and pumps his legs and sees himself running from the beach with Harvak at his side. The family stove floats in the ocean. *I'm going to see you again. I'm going to leave and get a chance to start over.* At the horizon the prison melts like stomped mud and a ring of light expands outward igniting the ocean in shark-fin flames. Harvak barks looking backward and leaps to the side from the following light. Mom stands in the front yard holding the cast iron pot rimmed in little green crystals. When Pants looks up, the sky is a mirror of all this, and he sees himself and Harvak become encased in light.

28

When Mom was a child she had an imaginary friend named Tock Ocki who only appeared in the corner of the bathtub when she was in the bathroom. He had a toddler's body and the head of a rabbit. Mom said the kids at school threw dirt in her eyes during recess and at lunch they said she would be alone forever. Tock Ocki told her that special people are destined to do special things. He stood in the tub, folded and unfolded his ears, and danced. She became so happy when he did this that she felt like she wanted to live forever.

27

It's a brittle corner soon to be dust. Pants shoves a sliver under his big toenail until it knifes the flesh. Pacing in his cell, he bends his toe inside his sneaker, the crystal cracking and cutting, slitting open skin. He prepares this way for the health meeting because he has to talk during the health meeting. It's difficult enough to listen to hundreds of words exiting a guard's mouth about god, but to return them sober among peers and the supervisor is nearly impossible. It's hard to look at people who have faces. Besides, he thinks he's leaving this place sometime soon and one last health meeting is doable.

The meeting takes place in the administrative wing, in the feet of the large L that is the prison. It's been quiet lately, inmates on the upper levels succumbing to the heat and whispering rumors that the city is moving mysteriously toward the village. No one, not the guards, not the prisoners, not the administration, knows what to believe, so they wait and stick to their schedules, which include the meetings.

A table with a coffee urn, Styrofoam cups, a cube of napkins, and a box of donuts is placed against the wall in the meeting room. In the center – eight white plastic chairs with metal legs. The floor is a smooth and slippery cement. One wearing socks could run through the open door of the room, glide to the opposite side, and bump into the guard who stands ready for the meeting, arms crossed high and tight, his expression absurdly serious.

Pants is ushered into the room by a guard who tells him to *get up on it*. Pants faces the cement block wall so close he smells the crystal fungus of his own breath. He stands in a wide stance with arms reaching for the corners of the ceiling, fingertips pressed into the stucco's dimples. Behind him, chairs arranged in a circle, the plastic boom of each put into proper place, metal legs scratching the cement, a guards keys jangling as he paces. The donuts are opened. A gravel-voice says, "Nice, donuts." The urn's orange tongue is flicked up, coffee rushes along styrofoam, and another voice, this one scary deep says, "Nice, coffee." A guard states there is a strict two-donut limit. He repeats himself, holding two fingers in the air while pivoting back-and-forth 180 degrees, because Tony, with his massive hand grabs five at once. The guard signals with his eyes to put the extra donuts back but Tony manages in one bite to taste all five.

The other guard squats, and holding McDonovan's calf with two hands, moves up his leg. His hair is inspected by a two-hand tousle that reminds Pants of Mom checking for lice – bugs they heard about from the city and never would have cared about but a panic ensued. They react to the policies of the city, especially if on television. He curls his big toe so the crystal touches the bottom of his shoe and the shard sinks in, hurts. When he extends the toe, blood and liquid crystal warms his foot, feels real good. When he closes his eyes, the guard's hands patting his hips (*ten times quickly, what are the chances of that*), he sees a beach with Remy running into waves colored night.

Goon-bodies plop themselves into the chairs. Everyone settles in. Everyone gets ready.

"Turn," says the guard who is the guard with the gold cross necklace, which appears several times larger than before, the gold cross now covering his chest and stomach.

"You got it, sexy hands," Pants says with his now usual goofy smile. He wants to make the guard feel uncomfortable and "sexy hands" does the trick.

"Op-en," says the guard. "Don't sass me. I said it before, the lord will decide and speak through Sanders."

"Touch me, hurt me, love me."

He opens his mouth and it's so clean that the guard takes a step back and peers up into the mouth. Those who eat black crystal are known to have black worm spirals rotting their inner cheeks. The tongue a block of coal. If the guard could see down McDonovan's throat he'd see pink fleshy walls draped in sheets of watery fungus, a symptom of a capable body flushing out the black after each use. Pants shuts his mouth, swallows, and the watery fungus washes away. He smiles without showing teeth. Has the smile of his mother.

"Good to go," the guard says. "Wait and see."

"That's what we're all doing, right?"

"Move."

"I mean, seriously, we're all just waiting for something to happen, to end us? That's what this life is?"

Sitting down, he rests his forearms on his thighs, slightly above the knees, and clasps his hands. He's dressed in orange pants and an orange top with a flimsy collar and two white buttons. His arms are long and skinny and losing muscle. His legs are thin too, not much below the knees swimming inside the orange material. His chest hurts when he coughs. The lights in the room suck up all space.

The supervisor is a big white guy with a block head and a military crew-cut named Jugba Marzan, commonly known as Jug, who wears high-waist khaki pants and a white button down shirt with the sleeves twisted sloppy at the elbows. He smells like hot dog water and mouth mints.

Not a guy who is completely out of shape, but looks like he played football and juiced and then let it all go. Sad.

Jugba says they will speak in an open and non-judgmental forum. The rules are simple. Everyone needs to say something about their past. Jug is allowed to ask two questions, after which, he will move to the next person.

"You. Say what you want, anything at all, this is a safe place where everyone, everyone *right*, will keep their opinions to themselves until everyone has had a turn. Things should run smoothly today. I'm under supervision myself," he looks up at a moving camera in the corner, "and the last thing I need is an incident like we've had here before. I'm in control. We're going to learn." Jug smoothes the chest of his shirt with two hands. He's incredibly nervous.

"…"

Everyone wears orange with white sneakers, black Velcro straps replace laces. A man named Crumb – small, mean – pinches the ashy tattooed praying hands on his neck while leaning back in his chair until the front legs hover off the ground, his cheeks puffed with air, his eyes blue and distant. There's Pete with his forearm tattoos inked in arial black – left arm: Everything I Kill I Fuck, right arm: Everything I Fuck I Kill – who chews watermelon flavored gum and crumples the tent of orange fabric at his crotch with a bouncing finger. Tony sits slumped, his arms larger than most men's thighs, folded over his chest, his left shirtsleeve rolled up above the bicep revealing a rash of raised skin in the shape of a key. Others sit looking at their shoes waiting for the health meeting to just end.

Jug has donut powder on his face. "All right, gotta play," he says, chewing his lips.

"…"

Pants shuts down when attempting to externalize emotion. This fact he's learned from these meetings. Something about family systems or was it family of origin. He stares at Jug. He leans forward. His big toe rubs the bottom of his shoe and his entire foot feels wet, hot, but he can't get moving. Not here.

Not like this. He can't enter the high because of their faces. The black crystal isn't strong enough for him to escape this time even though he's done it before on less. The obligation surrounding him is suffocating. Jug's question is drawing him out. Reality has a way of breaking you.

"Donut," says Jug. "Now speak."

" … "

Two invisible chambers floating in the center of the room are this: Jug asking Pants to talk, his chamber filling up, and the reaction chamber is Pants shuts off, the chamber emptying. They are connected. He knows this. Things learned. Basic Distancer vs. Pursuer. His emotions are hidden under crystals. He wants to flip the chambers and come out with so much hiss and words that Jug will blow back through the wall and dissolve. The black crystal rushes through his veins and creates bumps on his skin. There are no bumps on his skin, Pants just imagines them, but he starts rubbing his arms. He needs to get on the beach. It's getting stronger, he can feel it.

"Crystal shithead," says Crumb. "Go and we get this over with."

" … "

A guard circles holding a club in one hand, a cup of coffee in the other. He's eaten three donuts, smells like clean laundry, and has a chicken dinner waiting at home. He's one of the few guards who doesn't eat crystal and is against the other guards taking it. He's friends with the guard who wears the gold cross and together they pray in a room located in the prison used for nothing but praying. The praying room is labeled Praying Room. There's an oil painting of an illuminated Jesus and a carpeted kneeling bench in royal purple. They really love to pray. The other guards who are hooked on the black crystal dislike them for what they interpret not as personal belief, but a moral judgment on their souls. The guard looks around the room for something to attack.

Everything looks weird to Pants. The guard's eyes are a horizontal slit across his head which is a grape and the lights on the ceiling slither and drool. The air is pixilated. Tony's arm rash is raised and jellied. His chair feels hot and alive.

"Holy shit," says Jug.

" . . . "

"I think," says Crumb. "I'd eat the village cold."

Pants speaks. The story is this:

When he was nine years old he followed Mom into the mine.

He thought she was a witch because she wore a black robe. Seeing her without her usual gray gown reminded him of seeing Dad for the first time without a mustache – a cruel trick with paralyzing aftershock for a toddler. He followed her. She was a shadow in that black gown floating over the truck-pressed roads, past the vegetable stands, poorly constructed leaning shacks, homes with crude metal roofs, the loud-lighted bars with street corners gorged with drunks vomiting count. He followed her into the mine, keeping his distance in the dark. She performed a séance. Knees bent, body bouncing from side to side, she growled as she reached for the sky. She placed an invisible towel over the head of the moon and cleaned it. Years later he'd find out many mothers conducted séances to increase their count when they felt sick. It was normal. But what's not normal is her wearing a black robe instead of a gray gown. What's not normal is what happened to Mom and his reaction after and his following guilt.

"Well, okay," says Jug. "Good start. Weird. But discussing your childhood opens you up to the person you are now," he says repeating the words from a training manual. "Everyone see how that's good? You build on that."

Crumb and Tony check for more donuts and if the orange light is still lit on the coffee urn. With a swirling club the guard tells them to turn around.

Before Jug asks his first question, Pants says more. He speaks quickly, racing over the top-half of his words. Black robes walked into the mine. They tore the robe off Mom, and from where he was, his body flat, dirt in his mouth, trembling against the dirt, he watched them act in a way he had never seen before. He could have done something. He made fists.

Curl, straighten, curl, straighten. His big toe is a pumping valve. *Concentrate with calm.* The crystal sinks deeper and his ripped skin shrieks along a fuse behind his ears. *Finally maxed out.*

He sits up in the white plastic chair so straight it's freakish. He describes a man's measured punches through Mom's hands which moved like they were cleaning fog off a windshield. They took turns falling on her, pushing her body into the dirt, fucking her into deeper plateaus. The first man went back. Pants floods the room with words, eyes wet, the veins in his neck worm-thick and making even self-proclaimed tough-guy-Tony wince. His body needs to move. Usually he can jog in his cell where he imagines the beach and Harvak at his side. The worst part wasn't that he didn't stop the men, but that his dick got hard against the dirt and he slithered and he screwed the ground. His fists became caresses. Pete whispers into his hands cupped over his nose and mouth *What the fuck, dude* and Crumb defense-mechanism-laughs while shaking his head no.

"I returned to the mine and replayed what happened to Mom who never reported or said a thing about what happened to anyone and I would lay in the dirt and rock and push into it and I was messed up back then because I thought, I really believed that I would die from such thoughts, like a force would reach down and yank every crystal from my body like a spine or something and leave me there like that and I've thought afterward and being here in the prison I could have done something, banner, banner, banner, that Mom is so sick now cause of what happened and I didn't do anything, but I was a good boy, I didn't do anything wrong, and now Mom is sick cause of me and I just need to help her cause I'm good."

Pants stands and kicks the chair backward and it flips, the

soldered metal glob where the legs sprout from hits the guard's knees and he falls into a crossed-leg sitting position with a comical *Uhf.* Everyone else slides their chair back by extending their legs. Pants curls and uncurls his big toe. His foot is a puddle. Down the hall come extra guards. Pants keeps talking. He says he formed The Sky Father Gang to find answers on how to increase count, have Mom live forever, have Mom always be Mom, Mom as a god, until he stops, the inmates squeezing their fists looking back and forth, the guard rubbing his knees and standing with the cross in his mouth, the other, outside guards, wielding expandable batons turning the nearest corner, and Pants says to Jug who sits upright, eyes wide, a wet spot of sweat, or is it piss, *it can't be piss, jesus,* pooling from his stomach and through his khakis, "I wanted to save her but I didn't do anything" and tears stream from his eyes, "I could have done something but I didn't," and he readies, for the batons to open at the back of his knees, a ray of pain.

26

Behind rain clouds the sun looks like a giant daytime moon. The heat wave ignores the rain and refuses to leave. Holding old umbrellas, the elderly move through their daily tasks purchasing food from vendors and trading crystals they once worshiped for YCL, all the while worried – heads looking up, then left, then right, then down again and at their feet trudging through the muddy streets.

The truck drivers don't care about the sky or sun because they can get more work done in the rain. They dress in slick green rain robes. They wear crystals around their necks that dangle so low under their work shirts the chain links knot in their chest hair. Their heads are hooded by their rain robes and they drive fast. Tires spin smooth spitting water backward, the rain glistening off metal hoods, doors, the roofs of the trucks that enter and leave the mine a dozen times daily.

Senior driver, Skip Callahan, drives shirtless. He wears a yellow crystal headband instead of a green necklace. He has plenty of chest hair. Today, he's the lead truck in a line of ten making its return trip back into the mine. The first produced a few blue crystals, one green, lots of yellow, and a half of a dark red looking thing, all of it dumped in a field for workers to sift through. Men from the city once told Skip they'd be interested in buying the mine and Skip told them to get fucked. He slapped a fat face belonging to a politician named Sanders who rubbed his cheek while three others stood stunned. Skip knows other mine workers are potential sell-outs because of their personalities. They're willing to sell to save themselves from some unknown crushing. The sky thunders and the rain falls faster from cracks of lightning.

Skip loves the rain. He loves to work. He blasts the radio – a country song picked up via a city signal with lots of banjo and violin – and smokes cigarettes he rolls himself. His truck is immaculate. On both driver and passenger side floors is a square of torn cardboard he replaces when muddied. The glove box contains homemade cleaning supplies that slosh inside mason jars and a spiraled branch of dirty cloths covered in engine grease. The wind pulls the rain to the side as his truck bounces down the road. In the pale light, royal disc of sun above, two hands gripping the steering wheel, he grins white teeth.

Last night Skip sat in the dark of his bedroom with his hands balled up against his chest, an all too common crippling depression. His mother, who was extraordinarily healthy for her count (such skin), recently died from a truck accident. The villagers stood around slack jawed and terrified *(that's going to happen to me one day)* and watched her expel colors while Skip came running down the street, slowing as he saw the damage. He was told by a teenager that she was "hurt" in an "accident" and Skip thought he could help her, that maybe she had sprained a wrist or bruised a hip, anything but zero. He tried pulling her from the truck but that made her body worse, bend in unimagined ways, colors gushing from her chest. People winced and turned away. Since the accident he's found it hard to function outside of work. Work is his everything now. In the bedroom, Skip tried to concentrate on an image that made him feel joy and that was driving. There, he could move his hands. Using two flashlights, he created headlights on his bedroom wall and pushed his right foot forward into a pillow.

He drives, cigarette in his mouth, a long turn downward, foot resting on the brake pedal. He squints through the rain and sees two shadows in the distance, small and blurry, and so low to the ground Skip thinks they're either turtles or rocks. But as the truck straightens out from the end of the curved road, he notices it's two animals, dogs maybe, running directly at him. He tosses his cigarette out the window. The left side of his body gleams with rain. He extends his foot into the brake pedal. Too hard and the tires will dig up the hard crust the hot rain has created. The driver behind Skip flashes his lights and another in the pack blasts his horn. *Shitheads*, thinks Skip, and tries to slow the truck more but the front tires lock and skid.

He eases off the brake as the two dogs enter the headlights. He turns the wheel to the left, toward the towering wall of dirt, and the trucks behind follow in a motion smooth and centipede like. Skip is having difficulty seeing through the windshield. The combination of heat and rain and truck speed turn the headlights into smeared pearls. His CB radio crackles with *hey bud-e, we-with, you, every-thing okay, up-there-hey-oh-what-is-dat-whoa-um-Skip-easy-there-Skip-care-full.*

Ugly is the sky above the wall.

"What," says Skip into the rain-slashed windshield. He hits the wipers bar up but it's already all the way up.

Out the passenger window a dog runs past, legs caked in mud, tongue out, exposed teeth. One eye looks yellow, the other black. Keeping up with the dog is a child on all fours. A girl in red shorts. Blond hair cascades the length of her arms. She's incredibly fast and combined with how fast Skip is driving the dog and the girl blur past.

"Stop it or I'll – " says Skip, momentarily looking into the side mirror to see them vanishing into the rain. Then he concentrates back on the road and says, "Holy mother wow was that what," before driving the final section of the road down.

He reaches the bottom of the mine. The drivers circle around his truck. Crisscrossing headlights illuminate mine workers who wear black shorts, no shirts, and jog with wheelbarrows dirt-brimmed with crystals. Tonight's late-night undocumented batch will be sold to the city and used for engagement rings, special occasion earrings, displayed in New Age yoga studios, given to the hospital-sick for positive energy. They have their own crystals, but they don't have these crystals. Some will be sold to parents for their children who play a game called Lyfer, trade the crystals back and forth in a test of who can maintain closest to a hundred, the brightest colors worth extra. They hurry between the ringing bells of classes to lie about what they hold behind their backs and to trade furiously as teachers watch. Skip listens to the roar of truck engines shifting gears as he tries to comprehend what he just saw.

Ken Horgan, a rat-like man whom Skip has seen several times bleeding from the head after work shifts, rolls his window down. His neck turned back and up, eyes squinting in the rain, he says, "Whole-e-shit. Was that a werewolf?"

Skip drives a loop around the trucks. Gas pedal floored, the truck buckles through shifting gears. He heads back up and out of the mine on the road he just descended. Ugly is the sky coming over the wall. Skip wants to help because he is a person hardwired to help. He couldn't help his mom. Tires roll over the hand-prints over paw-prints. Ken Horgan says from the pit of the mine, standing in the rain with eyes like a rat being flicked with water, "COME BACK AND TELL ME WHAT THAT WAS SKIP I'VE NEVER KNOWN A HALF DOG PERSON BEFORE LET'S HAVE DINNER AND TALK ABOUT IT BUDDY."

Halfway to the house they stop because Hundred has something in his paw. He's been running on three legs. Remy, covered in mud, sits in the road and cradles him in her lap. The rain lets up to a spit. Steam places the village in a cloud and the lower half of the city disappears. She pulls out a triangle of dark crystal from his paw. Blood splatters across her fingers in a Z. His eyes break as his spine twists. Remy tries to say something like, "stop" but it comes out as "hop." He runs from her arms with impossible strength and Remy follows until they both enter the house.

"Hey, hop it."

"…"

"Hop it now."

They run up the stairs and down the hall, doors slamming shut behind. They jump into the tub. Remy turns the water on as Hundred play-bites her forearms. She laughs and can't believe he wants to be in the tub, he hates baths, but he seems to be loving it, barking and leaping and smiling the way dogs sometimes appear to be smiling. She slaps his body with both hands. More blood from his paw, a stream of numbers entering the water. He acts wild, his eyes bigger than all dog eyes combined.

Thud thud thud on the front door with a three second pause before another *thud thud thud*. They ignore it.

As the water splashes over her legs, rises above her stomach, the mud from Remy's skin and Hundred's hair washes off in black goops that she finger-paints on the tub's walls. Hundred eases into a calm state, but something is off. Remy has witnessed a transformation. Good, bad, she doesn't know yet, but something has happened. He's not acting happy anymore. She can't stop staring at the way he's moving, not like a dog, but like a bug on its back, trying to flip over and right itself. It's like he's trying to move inside himself or leave his own body.

"You okay?"

Hundred barks twice and turns his head to the thudding.

"Who's that?"

Before the water reaches her chest, Hundred leaps from the tub and leaves a wet slide of mud and dark goo extending out the bathroom, down the stairs, and to the front door where the thudding just won't stop.

"Hey, open up."

Hundred stretches his front legs up on the door and barks.

"I don't care what it is you're doing. I've known crystal heads before and it doesn't bother me, I just want to know if you are all right. Name is Skip and I work in the mine. I said, HELLO?"

Remy stays in the tub. Blood hangs from her feet. She sits back with the water at her chin and crosses her left foot over her right knee and inspects her foot. The air wobbles. She doesn't feel like herself anymore and that's a good thing. It's her birthday and later tonight Dad will shoot a single firework into the sky. Pressed into her skin are dark crystals. *Thud thud thud.* She picks one out and blood pours down her leg. They look black. Scared, where is Mom and Dad? What is this? She squeezes the crystal back in. A flash of heat travels from her foot to her head followed by a desire to run. The liquid retracts back inside her. Lifts her. She breaths in bursts and closes her eyes where she sees a body being carried to the mine where burned. Mom cried at the kitchen table this morning because when you guess how many are inside, you guess how many days you have left. Remy doesn't think about her lowering count because now she's at the opposite end of that thought. Here in the pink tub, the discovery of black crystal is an escalating number widening her veins, making her believe, making her become everything – plant, bird, horse, dirt, sun, Mom – alive.

There's one last series of knocks at the front door and then just Hundred barking, proud of himself for fighting off the knocks.

Skip Callahan stands shirtless in steam and rain. He only wanted to help. He turns and checks his idling truck. *What was that?* He walks back to his truck and looks at the fence. The city, like the sun, is way closer than yesterday. *What's happening?* The buildings are fanning out around them like cards. *I don't want to die*. People are walking the edge of the city. Some are using binoculars. Skip turns his back, lowers his pants, and jiggles his big body.

25

Lying under his sheet, he lifts his pelvis and builds a tent with his knees. He's coming down from peaking on black crystal and the beating he took at the health meeting. They hit his legs with sticks until he fell. He thinks about the letters from Mom and with his right hand rubs his stomach and shoots a beam of light from his bellybutton. Through the sheet and around the prison bars and into the village the light travels until it rests in triangular form on her bedroom floor. She dips the black crystal into the light. Twin horses rise on their back legs and kick holes in the ceiling.

24

As they struggle to position the table Z. stands on it and shouts at the sun. His face is dark with shadows and sweat. His green robe is strapped tight by his arms. Everyone is excited by this new project. Once the table is in proper place, according to Z., they sit down.

Trucks, wagons, bicycles, the few cars in the village, become a fat U shape of traffic forced to flow around them. A man driving a truck who is shirtless and smoking a hand-rolled cigarette lays on the horn. He reverses his truck and accelerates before stopping inches from the table. Arnold tells Skip easy, says to keep his cool. He reverses and accelerates again and again. It's a tactic to psyche the Brothers out that doesn't work. Skip is drenched from the rainstorm, his eyes crazed, his hair matted to his forehead in the shape of a bird's gray wing.

"Easy, Skip, easy," says Arnold. "Look like you've seen Royal Bob!" Arnold waits for someone to laugh but no one laughs.

Red globs stretch then drip from the rim of the sun.

"Skip, come on now," says Ricky. "No need, no need."

"I got this," says Z.

Everyone stops and looks at Z. who somehow appears more natural standing on a table as opposed to sitting. He runs the length of it, huffing dramatically, moving his arms robotically, legs like pistons, and everyone leans back as he leaps from the edge of the table and lands in a crouched position on the truck's hood. His feet crumple metal. He screams at Skip with a pointed finger and says he's trying to enjoy his dinner and Skip, head down, head filled with images of a dog-child, and not really looking at Z., he hates Brothers Feast, but still looking up slightly just enough to see him, dislike him, holds up a hand and mouths *okay*. When Z. walks back across the table he glances in Bobby T.'s direction, shrugs his shoulders, and smirks like a child reaching into a drawer.

"S-s-s-sorry, Bobby T.," he says. "I'm s-s-s-stressed."

He dance-walks, hips humping in the direction of the sun, and the Brothers, not knowing what to do exactly from this new behavior, drum the table.

"Hey," says Bobby T., "it's been hard."

Which is true. Z. has wrecked his mind trying to define the jailbreak in reverse. He's close. They're close. The time spent defining the jailbreak doesn't matter because once it's completed no one will ask how long they spent working. You're remembered for your actions not your planning. People who are remembered are remembered forever because they travel in memories, from old to young, and what's greater than that. What's greater than living forever and not being alive to see the consequences.

"I'm this close," says Z. and holds his thumb and pointer finger a quarter inch apart before sitting back down. "That means really close," he adds.

A bag of hot air in the sky moves like an ameba. The Brothers have dinner by candlelight at the table in the street. Inside the bag, the ameba, thousands of tiny things are moving and it's only Z. who looks up, smiling and admiring the strangeness of this sky creature.

"SMART ASSES," someone says. It's one of the mine workers. "We should sell and be done with this nonsense. They will take over no matter what, just look at the buildings, you dolts." A crowd of Brothers Feast supporters including Ken Horgan shoves the mine worker away, down the street, as he continues to shout backward over his shoulder about the end of times, their imminent destruction resulting in nothing but city.

Another mine worker says, "Nice... *reeeeaaal* nice. They are laughing at us every day and this, what does this do to help?"

The Brothers have no reaction. They enjoy their dinner in the street.

A man outside a bar reaches into a rusty barrel and extracts a turkey leg. With a big swinging arm he launches the leg skyward, toward the stretching bag, the ameba in the sky. The turkey leg lands on the table and wobbles their plates. They thank the man and portion off the gristle-rot. Men and women in their traditional robes, their backs hunched from mandatory years working in the mine boo the Brothers with spittle.

"Just working on our public image," Bobby T. tells the crowd.

"Quiet and obedient is what we need," says Ricky.

"It makes sense to be disciplined," says Z. "Don't act weird, right, right."

They all smile and nod and eat. They drink coffee from a metal urn kept hot by the air. The sweat on their skin thickens to a clear goo that traps lightweight bugs. Z. takes a long drink from his mug. He notices one bug has a sucking mouth and he leaves it there, sucking, on his wrist.

A woman in an orange robe runs up and slaps the cup from Z.'s hand. The coffee paint-splatters Ricky's sleeve. The cup rolls across the table and falls to the ground while Z. sits frozen, mouth open, pretending to still hold the cup until the woman walks away mumbling, calling him a lost child.

"The s-s-s-service here is *awful*," says Z. and everyone laughs. He heard the "lost child" comment and it hurt. He just needs to define the jailbreak in reverse and his life will work out. Everything that has become before will be nothing.

Daylight wastes to dark. Residents retreat to their homes. The Brothers stay at the table in the street, candles flickering, the bag of hot air in the sky, the moving ameba, pops and pours millions of locusts, black bugs, bugs with sucking mouths, invisible tiny things with just wings. The Brothers barely notice, they look at the city. Another building is on fire. Village radicals known as Black Mask are trying to stop the city's growth by burning sections. This has happened several times and no one in the village is sure who is doing it exactly, but it's most likely two or three mine workers. Some think it's Royal Bob, running in his blue shorts, his long gray hair burning and swatting the base of the buildings. But no one believes burning buildings will stop the city. For every building burned to the ground, three more rise in its place.

Full dark from above. They stay up with the heat figuring out what the jailbreak in reverse is. Z. reads over the letters received from the prison. There's a new one that he somehow missed and Z. blames Arnold for the letter being placed in the old, already read piles. Arnold's skin burns so bad from the heat he thinks he's covered in biting bugs and he slaps his arm. There are bugs, tons of them, on him. He apologizes. Z. reads the letter once, twice, then three more times, holding it up with two hands. He cross-checks it with several letters and notes, then goes back to this new letter. Arnold notices, his nose practically touching his arm, that little bugs, barely visible, are burrowing into him.

Z. shouts, "I GOT IT," and startles Arnold and the others.

He's covered in glistening sweat.

He's shaking and smiling and holding the paper with two hands like he's looking through it and into the sky and he screams again, "I-I-I DID IT I GOT IT I ACTUALLY DID IT Y-Y-Y-YOU FOOLS DID YOU HEAR ME I-I-I GOT IT."

They finalize the plan that will free The Sky Father Gang and make Z. forever known. It's all he's ever wanted. As a child he spent eight days looking for a turtle because he heard they existed, came from the city. He never wanted something so bad. His mom ended up getting one from Mob of Mary's and it died three days later. When he stands on the table again it's not with anger, but joy. He carves circles in the air with his fingers and gyrates his hips. Streams of burning turquoise rain down a curve in the sky. Arnold slaps the table and Ricky and Scotty and Bobby T. mouth-fart a beat and shout, "Yeah! Yeah! Yeah!" They dance and celebrate and swat bugs from their faces until the sun comes up, the temperature rising, the future as them in it, forever.

23

With a screwdriver from Dad's toolbox Mom chisels off a piece of black crystal, why not. She listened for years to her son speak about increasing count (life, longer). He once walked home with the first black crystal and gave it to her. She didn't know he had others. She didn't know he would experiment and form something as dangerous as The Sky Father Gang. She should try something, anything, even if she doesn't believe in it, yes, even if she doesn't believe in it because the meaning of life is to feel some good even though what's inside you is a waiting zero. She moves the screwdriver.

Mom has okay days and bad. At her worst, she stays in bed where she coughs crystals into the spitting cloth (Chapter 2, Death Movement, Book 8). Her number skims a green lake, dives, and tadpole-swims away from her. During her okay days Mom sits in the triangle of sunlight entering her window and warms her face for hours. At the dinner table she acts in a way that doesn't turn Remy's head in the opposite direction. But most days are bad. Under the covers at night she traces with her finger the sharpness of her hipbones and imagines a man fitting both hands around her as if she were a clay pot, lifting her up, and drinking what liquid is left.

She moves the screwdriver over the black crystal trying to peel it apart.

The family has broken apart over the years in a honeycomb hexagon of ways. That's how she sees it – a solid shape but with separate pieces inside. She remembers the night in the mine, the men. They were dressed like mine workers. She didn't speak to anyone about what had happened. The distance between herself and her husband is an endless black field, their bodies as shadows inside the black field moving away from each other, neither able to see the other. She didn't want to be touched after it happened and Dad's hand-on-hip move in the kitchen was viciously swatted away. She told herself, or was it Dad, she could push the experience away, and with time, destroy it.

She places the piece, which is the size of a clipped toenail, under her tongue. It's sharp and with any movement will sink in. She sits on the floor in the sunlight triangle. She considers trying for the Horses Hologram again, and in the thought, doesn't realize she's chewing the crystal, breaking it into specks, and swallowing.

It's a good amount of black crystal to take. When a hot flash blankets her body she inspects her arms because they feel swollen. There's the tadpole-swimming-away-from-her feeling again but this time it's pleasant and warm. Her body is at first underwater, then exploding out of the water and into the sun. Heat, a hard ball of it, rolls up from her stomach and clogs her throat. She screams, laughs, sees herself running the circumference of the earth. She swallows and the lump in her throat flattens. Mom thinks she's added and with one finger she taps her chest and counts to fifty. She smiles into the sun with her eyes open, blinding, not caring. On thirteen pieces of paper she writes

I'm not sick anymore.
I'm not sick anymore.
I'm not sick anymore.
I'm not sick anymore.
I'm not sick anymore.
I'm not sick anymore.

I'm not sick anymore.
I'm not sick anymore.
I'm not sick anymore.
I'm not sick anymore.
I'm not sick anymore.
I'm not sick anymore.
I'm not sick anymore.

and throws them into the air before she feels an insatiable need to move.

She walks from her room and through the hallway with beige paint peeling and family portraits with green crystal-studded frames melting. It's impossible to lose her balance, she feels so good, so she skips on one foot for several steps, laughing, until walking again, hands tracing waves on both walls. She stops at his room in one big jump.

Dad sits on the bed, pillows propped up behind him, his legs extended. He wears a pair of white underwear with blue trim. His body is sprouted with black hair, his skin tan and cracked. He is sad, quiet, tired. From the uncovered ceiling light his body glistens. She asks why things are so difficult. He sighs dramatically. Mom isn't acting like Mom, asking him more questions, brimming with energy. What can she do so Remy doesn't grow up to be like her Brother? Is she bad? Tell her she's not. Tell her things like bathing her children in the kitchen sink, and breastfeeding them every hour, and walking them for miles inside their home to sleep, and comforting them through endless cries, and trimming their nails while they squirm, and massaging little constipated bellies, and walking slanted from exhaustion, bruising her arms on doorways, and not bathing for a week, and eating all meals over the kitchen sink, eyes and mind always on her babies, everything for her babies, never putting herself first, tell her it meant something.

"Talk," she says, not sounding like Mom. "Say anything."

Hundred barks through the walls and Dad smiles thinking how they tried hiding him.

"Please," says Mom. "I need you to."

She moves her weight from one foot to the other, her heavy blood shifting inside her from leg to leg. She can't stop her twitching fingers. Her eyes burn undiscovered colors.

"Did you actually have the energy to make that cherry pie?"

"Cherry," she says. "You bought it days ago at Sheperds. Do me a favor."

"You're a good mother," he says getting up from the bed. He doesn't want to be bothered with words. The worst thing you can do to Dad is trap him and only allow an escape by conversation. He's so limited. It's unfair to him and more unfair to Mom.

"One favor," says Mom.

"She's smart, she'll be fine. Not everything needs to be discussed all the time."

"All the time."

"See, right there."

"This isn't about you. Can you do something for me?"

He stands in his underwear, and she stands in her gray nightgown, both under the light. Paint is peeling around the edges of the window where the heat enters. Even the floor feels heated. She puts her arms around his body and rests her head on his chest. He can't remember the last time they touched like this and the gesture, after sending an initial shock through his body that makes him move one step backward, then seems to soften him, his body going back against hers, makes his hands move up and through her hair.

"What is it?"

"Just move a little," she says.

He squeezes her gently around her upper back and swallows her smallness. He envisions a life without her, living in this heat with Remy, and thinks how a family isn't a family with just a daughter and a father. You need higher numbers. He's going to lose her. Each strand of her hair is coated in sweat. He hums, and together their hips sway and he says yes, her children remember everything, that's their job, to keep remembering.

22

He found a bird with a broken wing. He stepped on the broken wing with one foot, and stepped on the good wing with his other foot. He moved his toes away from the bird's body until a bone cracked. Remy told him to stop. He smeared her wings across the dirt. This was the worst thing he ever did as a child. The bird exhaled her final crystal in a circle of knotted smoke.

21

Remy walks into the mine before the workers arrive. Her bare feet slog through mud created by the heat wave rain. Steam rises from the ground in a prehistoric kind of way. Over her dirty red shorts with white trim she wears a purple nightgown taken from Mom's closet. *Smells like old person.* She imagines walking through younger ghost-versions of herself *(how many times have I walked into this mine?)* and swats them away, sprints, shouts at them, plays spit-tag with them. She's at the mine for one reason and one reason only.

In a plastic bucket she collects a dozen black crystals. They exist. Dug up by a truck's tires during the rainstorm. They've been here all this time, beneath everyone's noses who never looked close enough and just needed the perfect combination of temperature and rainfall to unlock the mud. Her bare feet helped, the workers with their thick boots are useless. Black crystals slide around the plastic bucket Remy holds. The sun is a bully on her shoulders, pushing her head down, face to chest. The sun highlights the black crystals and she fills the bucket and runs home.

In her bedroom she breaks them into shards with a hammer taken from Dad's toolbox. On the floor she forms a black box. She steps in barefoot and marches. *It don't hurt.* She shouldn't be doing this, but ever since running in the mine with Hundred and cutting her feet, sitting in the tub and getting sky-high, she's been craving the sensation. Remy believes she's discovered a way to live longer. *Each crystal inside me births a twin.* The broken crystals slice her feet until her legs end at the ankles.

She jumps up on the bed and pulls her left foot up to her mouth and picks each crystal out then puts them back in. She does this foot, then the other, and goes back and forth in a blur until she can't do it once more, her arms sore like lifting buckets of YCL, helping Dad and Brother. Under her bed it smells like vomit. She stretches out and goes giddy with anticipation. Her body hums. When she places her hands on her stomach she ascends and the black crystal drawn on the ceiling inflates with light. Mom says something from her bedroom. Her body is kept together by disease. Her wrists are the diameter of a broom handle. Remy has had a repeating nightmare for a week of a game show where Mom is a table made of slush she has to carry down a staircase. The surrounding audience, wearing raincoats and green casino visors, hold signs that read ZERO MAMMA. Remy always trips and launches table-Mom skyward to the audience leaning away.

Remy remembers those who came from the city – meaner looking compared to the soft faces of Mob of Mary's – selling stolen televisions, the white price tags still on, dangling in the dark. They had heard of these machines before and the box of light in person was real seductive. Dad said okay, wanting to do something special for the family but hating having to engage in these kinds of forced interactions. They bought one with a long metal antennae the sellers seemed to mock. They tried to get him to buy a more expensive one. But it worked just fine – Dad adjusting the wire V into a position so you couldn't leave the room without knocking it over. The shows they watched didn't relate to them at all but the colors were pretty and the actors' voices always loud and stories engaging. For a full year, once a week, they watched a show about a family living on a beach near a forest. The family used their stove as a boat to catch fish. Remy and Adam couldn't stop asking Mom and Dad what an ocean was, why couldn't they have one, what's a turtle, why does the moon pull the ocean, what's a jellyfish, does sand burn.

Black crystal doesn't last long in teenagers. It's leaving her system but she's still seeing the new.

Sensation reenters her feet as Remy floats down from the ceiling draped in dogs. Hundred is wrapped around her neck like a scarf. Harvak, sinking into her chest, tells her no one will live much longer, this life is constantly ending, it's her job to save Mom. Remy says she knows, it's what she's going to do, stop choking me, if this life is constantly ending, then it's constantly beginning.

20

Driving in his truck at night, thinking about treating Remy with more kindness, *don't be so short with her, she's just a girl, you understand how hard she has it, she can name her dog whatever* he hits something that crumples the hood into a pile of tents.

The sound of the accident can be heard in the city and some run to The Bend with their binoculars.

His body hugs the steering wheel. His head touches the windshield which is the hood. Smoke rises from the headlights and the engine hisses. The tires on the left side go flat and Dad leans. When his arms slide off the steering wheel he jolts up with a loud gasp.

Hands on his chest, he exhales and coughs blue slush. Dad inspects his arms, chest, stomach, and thighs. No sign of blood or crystals leaking out from these parts, but from inside, yes, some organ split open. On the rearview mirror is a honeycomb hexagon in thin black marker with the words THIS IS WHAT OUR FAMILY IS LIKE written across it. *Remy how dare you what's the matter with you.* She's been acting strange, someone not Remy moving inside Remy, someone not the same daughter he sat with wearing floppy robes, talking his heart out.

He rolls his neck and practices breathing. His ribs are sore at each inhale and he's reminded of the last time the wind was knocked out of him – in the only fight of his life – by a kid in The Sky Father Gang. Dad wanted to talk to his son before he went into the city. Dad wanted to tell him not to go, maybe it was his fault he was acting this way, how about we try talking this out. The kid with the black crystallized facial scar in the shape of a key said his son didn't want to talk and aimed his fist for the backside of Dad's heart and landed.

When he opens the door, his knees and hands hit the ground. He crawls to the front of the truck. What he drove into is a table with dinner plates, melted candles, and a turkey leg with little meat. Dad massages his calves. His jeans are covered in dirt and some YCL from a mason jar that was to be added to the home generator. They've been running low lately and Dad is worried they will run out. It takes him ten minutes to stand.

"Hey, you. What you doing out here?" says a girl, a runaway, in purple spiked shoes. She smokes a cigarette awkwardly, her T-shirt looks shredded, and she stands in the glow of a break light.

"What am I doing out here?" says Dad. "What are YOU doing out here?" He spits up more blue slush and the girl steps back. "GET. NOW. OUT OF HERE."

The girl runs toward the fence, back to the city.

"NO ONE FROM THE CITY BELONGS IN THE VILLAGE," shouts Dad. "STAY AWAY." Then, even though he knows it's impossible, "I'M TELLING YOUR PARENTS ABOUT THIS." His chest hurts from the words coming out and he imagines a jagged crystal now lodged across his lungs.

He leans inside the truck and turns the key, his breathing sharp and painful. Nothing. Key frozen. His hand slips in blue slush covering the key. The mason jar with the YCL is empty and shattered and he notices another patch of blue slush where he sat. He calculates he probably lost several. For a few minutes he sits sideways in the truck, his legs dangling out, not sure what to do, how to explain this, how to lie. Maybe just be honest with her. What was he thinking. He could run into the city, it's so close, but the accident is a red flag indicator of worse things to come. Besides, now he's remembering the history of those who have entered the city, all those consequences, that prison. What was he thinking. That he could seriously drive in, sleep in his truck, eventually sell it, and start over as a man who wore a suit? He stands up and slams the door closed but it doesn't fit anymore, appears to be the door to a much smaller vehicle, and bounces right back into his hand.

Dad looks for the moon as he walks home but sees only a massive black circle with a thin white border.

You can't help someone who is too sick for help. There is no meaning in the offer when you should have done something before. You should worry about yourself and Remy now.

He walks into his wife's room. She sits on the floor holding a red box.

"I had an accident taking a drive," he says, undressing. "A table, in the street. I'm okay. I'm not hurt, so no need to worry, no need to get worked up."

Mom stands and needles pour down her legs (Chapter 3, Death Movement, Book 8). She rubs his arms. She appears shorter. The bedroom has taken on more of a grave-yellow hue, like the bathroom, from the heat.

"Why were you out so late?"

A black smudge left by the steering wheel horizons his forehead. She touches it and he moves her hand away. She goes back again and he lets her.

"Wanted to clear my head. Isn't it strange that a table, *a table*, was in the middle of the street? I'm not talking about a piece of junk someone threw out. I'm talking about a full size dining room table. Kids. Brothers Feast. Black Mask. Royal Bob."

"You ever talk to Maggie next door? She told me the buildings are moving closer with the sun and it's the end of times. I know, she's old, don't listen to her with that voice of hers. But everything moves inward. We okay?"

"I'm fine. What's in the box?"

"Where were you driving?"

"A really big table."

"You were driving to where you could see the prison, weren't you," says Mom, stepping closer, voice lowering a little, forcing eye contact. "Like we used to do. Don't look at me like that. Don't be the hard you, you were so gentle with me before, be like that. Remember sitting in the truck and watching the lights turn on at the prison and imagining that our thoughts were matching up with his thoughts? I do."

He looks at his boots dotted with specks of blue. He immediately becomes worried that he's lost more than just a few. He immediately becomes conscious that he's moving toward zero, and as fast as the thought arrives, he rejects it. "Truck is wrecked."

"I remember thinking I was kissing his forehead and hoped he was thinking of me kissing his forehead."

"I'm not going anywhere. Nothing has changed." He studies the gauntness of her face and tries to locate the past her with his finger.

"Nothing has changed," she repeats and shakes her head away from his hand. Outside there's that sound bugs make when it's too hot and another building burning. The firemen wear pearl-colored heat-resistant suits and shine like soap bubbles as they fire hopeless streams of water from long hoses kids stomp on. "Can you say how you're feeling? Why has it been like this for years and years and years and I just put up with it? I know that look, you don't want to get into this. And don't tell me it's because of the separate beds thing. It's always been this way. We'd drive out and look at the prison and I cried and said everything I felt but you never said anything. You just kind of sat there. Numb and cold."

Then Dad blurts out, "Okay, I considered leaving."

It's difficult for her to stand without the black crystal fully in her bloodstream. Her legs are stilts. She's taken more of it, but it's leaving her system again and she's losing the energy for everything. She's not fully shocked by what he says, but it still hurts.

"I was going to drive as far away as possible. I wanted out. I couldn't take it anymore. Sometimes it all feels so unlivable."

"Would have been easier to leave than watch me die. Where's my cloth? I have the worst dreams now."

Dad speaking at her back as she moves around the bed: "I thought that. I've thought about a life by myself and thought how much easier – "

Mom lies down in bed. Dad stands next to the bed.

"Why didn't you?"

"Why didn't I?"

"Why didn't you walk in? You could have made a life selling crystals, running back and forth and grabbing the best ones."

"Did you just say there's a problem with your dreams?"

She spits on the chest of her nightgown. The goo shines with red crystal or thick blood. Dad circles the bed, an ache in his lower back developing from the accident that will only get worse from now on. He wants to change the subject away from what he's feeling. She seemed so much stronger before, when they held each other and he hummed that song.

"Remy talks about dying."

"We've talked about it," says Mom. "The city, the sun, but she can't discuss death?"

"She's small."

"Not thinking about dying is living in denial," says Mom, touching the liquid on her chest. "My legs hurt."

"I'm not going anywhere."

"You were."

"If I didn't care, I wouldn't have come back."

"You know those television shows that go really fast to zip through a scene, and it's funny? Like that show we watched with the family who lived on the beach? I see us like that, but it's not funny. It's just the two of us moving to opposite sides of the house and the house is shrinking. His imprisonment changed us but we never talked about it enough. I saw it in you the first time we sat in the truck, watching. You were damaged. You should have gotten it out of you back then but you didn't."

"I don't know. How am I supposed to respond to that? Anything I say is going to be unhelpful. I don't have anything to say."

"You don't have to."

"I care about you and Remy more than anything."

"I think the most selfish people are the quietest." More spit, a deeper shade of red. "Promise you won't leave again. I need you here. We do. What do you think it's like to be zero?"

"I don't know."

"Maybe it's like the city."

"Concrete and endless noise?"

"Wonder if I'll feel anything."

"Phones, politicians."

"Wonder if it smells like anything."

"Does that matter?"

"They have a hospital."

"I'm not going anywhere," says Dad, and comes back to her and sits on the edge of the bed and rubs her legs in long deep strokes that she doesn't notice. He loves her, but can't handle what is happening because he can't control it. Later, he'll walk to the kitchen for the spitting cloth. It will be the last time – the cloth the texture and color of smashed cherries disintegrating over his hands as he rinses it out. He wants to ask her again about her dreams. He wants to know what's wrong with them.

"I can't feel you."

Part Two

19

He receives a letter from Brothers Feast saying the jail-break in reverse has been finalized and they are coming into the prison. He's traded letters with Z. and they've worked together on the escape plan and everything is ready. McDonovan knows breaking in is risky, teetering on the absurd, but it's worth it because there's a chance he will see his family. Mom wrote there's a new dog named Hundred who has one yellow eye and one black. She and Dad haven't been getting along (nothing new) and something about a truck accident in the street (truck wrecked, bad back). In his reply letter he asks for a specific date and time, wondering how they could forget something so crucial.

She's tried the black crystal and the sensation is an illusion to a rising number. Black crystal foams your eyes with what you think are crystals stacking inside your body, the pyramid growing, but it doesn't hold. At first she felt better from her sickness, but later, the rush of illness flooded back stronger. He wrote *And everyone wants to live longer, how sad. I will see you guys soon. There's been talk of my release. Love and all things good, Adam.* She touched his name.

Pants is escorted by a guard through the prison's exercise room and into the basketball court. Inside his left shoe his foot is bandaged from the destruction of his big toe, the shard of black crystal that ate away the nail and much skin during the health meeting. The guard tells him to stop dragging his feet by tapping his club on the back of his thighs.

Today is a privilege day. This occurs about once a month. Administrators have inmates use the basketball court, run a track outside, or allow a one-hour session in the gym with light weights. There's a rumor about a swimming pool, but Pants has never been taken because the follow-up rumor is that someone drowned in the swimming pool, the body quickly disposed of, wrapped in painter's plastic and tossed into the afternoon garbage truck.

Two steel doors painted white open. He's pushed inside, the guard kind of shrugging when Pants gives him a look back. The doors close with a clang followed by a second clang that is the lock. The floor is shoe-scuffed parquet. A layer of shellac seals dents and gives glare. The single basketball hoop is a transparent charcoal-dusted backboard with red rim, no net, which is attached to a cement wall. Glued on all four walls are six-foot-high sections of cushioned matting in gray, red, and blue. The ball sits under the hoop and Pants jogs slowly, his white shorts riding up, and grabs it.

His first shot is a fourteen-foot jumper with no arc that arrows through the no-net. He runs to the ball that bounces off the padded wall. Sneakers squeak with each sharp but careful turn. Pants, on the baseline, drives in for a lay-up while a guard with a head like a hamburger looks in from a window above. He takes more shots, lost in thoughts of childhood because his only future thought has been breaking out and seeing his family again and he can't think about it anymore, when it will happen or not. He's been putting together his childhood memory by memory. One shot comes close, bounces high off the back of the rim and nearly hits one of many spinning fans. The guard looking in shakes his head and blows on his lips.

When Pants McDonovan was a child he didn't use toilet paper.

He'd pull his underpants up, and using three fingers, wiggle them into the fabric, into his ass, and once there, curl-pick his fingers until assumed clean. In his bedroom, he'd take the underwear off and roll the soiled pair into a tube he hid in a dresser drawer. This continued until Mom noticed his lack of underwear in the laundry. She walked into his bedroom late one night with an armful of clean laundry and opened the bottom dresser drawer and found fourteen perfectly aligned rolls of dirty underwear. When she picked one roll up she noticed another beneath. The smell was so strong she thought Pants would wake, so she hurried from the room and into the bathroom where she unfolded the underwear revealing a wide splotch of dried shit in the shape of a hammered butterfly. She turned the sink on, let them soak in hot water, and tried not to feel that she had done something irreversibly wrong as a mother. She would confront him in the morning. She wouldn't sleep that night.

He said he didn't know why he did what he did, but boy it felt good, toilet paper was rough and sometimes didn't flush because the water pressure was so weak in their house. Their plumbing is city plumbing a hundred years ago. This is something the city knows and makes fun of. Men in city bars like to talk about how dirty the villagers are. It's another reason why the city should continue building. Just look at them, men in city bars say. They don't shower. They lie in rocks and mud and make babies in the mud. They don't worship a god. Mom said none of that mattered because what he did was wrong and it had to stop.

Dad couldn't look him in the eyes. He let Mom deal out the punishment. Grounded for a week. No play time in the mine with Remy. Also, forced to wash all his underwear to an insane brand new clean. The task taught him how to do laundry better than all, something he was strangely proud of but didn't tell anyone else about until the prison. But the punishment didn't work because Pants continued the habit and found new places to hide his dirty underwear: between his mattress and bedspring, between the window and screen with the blinds drawn, in a shoebox kept in the closet, behind the YCL generator in the basement, and finally, and best, behind his dresser.

He skipped school once a week to make the trip – a somewhat long walk from one side of the village to the other – to get the same kind of underwear his Mom bought with a matching design consisting of a red elastic band and bubble-words written across the crotch and backside that said WINNER. CHAMPION. VICTORY. They were different because they came from the city, traded for crystals curious city-folk displayed in their homes or taken from Mob of Mary's who always had a steady supply. He used these pairs not to wear, but to throw into the dirty laundry after he purposefully dropped them on the ground, dragging them through dirt and weeds.

But the room took on the bottom-drawer smell. The bright yellow paint above the dresser turned to the shade of straw. At first Mom blamed the moon, an unusual lighting effect caused the paint to look that way, but the smell couldn't be ignored and her denial wasn't strong enough. She wanted to believe that her words, her punishment, had been received and she was not only a good mother but an effective one who was developing her son to be a greater person than her and Dad. Again, she went into his room, this time when he was at school. She opened each drawer before pulling the dresser from the wall where a heap of underwear spilled to the sides, the paint behind the dresser peeled off in curling sheets, half a dozen brittle hooks fingering the air.

"I mean, how *ridiculous*. No more spending time with those boys. I'm telling your father. I don't know what to do with you."

What was said between parents: slightly worse than a spanking. Something to be remembered. He sensed the beating coming from Dad's truck heading home from the mine. He had never seen Mom so angry and had overhead the word *belt*. Even her cough was angry. He feared bruises. What he did to protect himself was take the rolled up dirty underwear on the floor and stuff it down the inside of his pants, covering his legs front and back. He put the underwear under his shirt and fattened his belly. He positioned underwear on his shoulders and became a little anxious monster waiting for Dad's anger to liquefy out and onto his body.

He lay on the bed with his chest rising and falling in the silence of the bedroom.

Mom greeted Dad in the driveway. Pants startled when Dad slammed the truck's door. Then he heard their voices through the window before they decided to go for a walk. Pants got up, kind of penguin-shuffled with the shit-underwear covering him and watched from the window until they came back up the road. He thought maybe nothing would happen. He thought maybe a big body wouldn't hurt his small body. A walk meant things were okay. Walks relaxed. You talked and felt better after a walk.

Again, they stood in the gravel driveway talking closely, the wind sweeping dirt from the road into brown wings against the sky above them. When Mom looked up at his window he fell backward and onto the bed and began hyperventilating. He couldn't control his air. The bed squeaked and he tried to calm himself down by saying it would be okay. Would it be okay?

Remy woke from her nap and shouted *Wake me up!*

His body felt miniature because the bed felt like it was the size of the room.

His breathing hurt.

Mom lifted Remy from the crib and she stopped crying.

Footsteps in the hallway.

A drawer being opened then closed.

Someone in the bathroom.

A body near the door.

Footsteps.

Then no footsteps.

When the door opened a hole opened in his heart.

Dad lunged in. The belt extended from his fist and hung against his thigh. His work shirt was stained with long drips of YCL and he smelled like mold. Pants sat up in bed, swung his legs over the edge, fell to his knees on the carpet scattered with underwater, and apologized. Mom said from the doorway maybe he would learn something this way because she had tried everything else. Her father had done the same to her, and so did Dad's, and it worked, look at them, adjusted people. She didn't necessarily believe what she thought, but her family history was stronger than her head. The important thing was a punishment that he would remember.

Going in for a lay-up that won't go in because Pants is directly under the rim, he understands Dad was so mad that day because of Mom. The fights, the silence at dinner, all things he saw but couldn't process, building up inside Dad, exploding against his boy's body. What was said during the walk was what upset Dad, and because he couldn't vocalize then, to her, what he felt, it came out against him. Why Mom allowed it he wasn't sure. It was so unlike her. He's not sure who is more at fault. He's not sure what it's like to be a parent, how difficult it is, all the mistakes made even though a parent is constantly trying not to make mistakes. But maybe that's the problem.

He can't make a single shot because his mind is in the bedroom.

He was lashed across the back of his legs and down his arms. Rolls of dirty underwear falling from his shirt in a strange and terrible magician *ta-da!* kind of way. One pair, from his left leg, wrapped around his ankle and stayed there for the remainder.

"I'm sorry," he babbled.

Dad flung him into the ceiling when he tried to hide in the space between wall and bed.

"I'm saying I'm sorry why aren't you stopping please why aren't you stopping?"

Dad grabbed his hand and dragged him to the center of the

room, the belt a blur, difficult for Pants to predict where the next hit would strike. The buckle landed in his palm and produced a rectangular welt.

"Enough," said Mom.

Dad kept going. The belt discovered new skin to plant bruises. But Pants wasn't trying to run away anymore. He was holding on to his father because he thought being close enough would make him stop. It appeared that he was trying to hug him, to get so close that the beating would *have* to stop and the only option would be an embrace. But it didn't work because Dad couldn't stop himself, everything emotional pouring through his swinging arm, his limbs buzzing with blood, everything coming out and onto his screaming son crumpled around his thighs, arms loosening with each strike down.

After Dad drove off in the truck Mom told her son to take off his shirt. She inspected his body. She was too shy to tell him to take his underwear off, but she never would have made it. His back was divided thirteen times in thirteen places. Stomach puffy and red, and in one area, split and bubbling crystal puss. All doors were shut now. Smelled like dead dogs, but mostly shit because his sweat had warmed the underwear that didn't fall out. Mom just stared at his heaving and bloodied back, the back that had once unfolded out of her. She sat on the couch. She couldn't stop thinking about his birth, the exact moment of it, and she connected it to this moment. He walked over and pulled her hands from her face.

"How many did I lose?"

She always told him a bedtime story about the sun leaving the sky because it had to visit the other side of the world and that night she told it to him in extended form, detailing villagers who ate light, rode crystal-armored horses, fought city workers in misty green mountains, until he fell asleep and she walked from the room, leaving him to the images, his recovery dreams. Mom stopped herself from feelings when Dad came home.

They didn't talk. She lay in bed pretending to be asleep and hoping he wouldn't smell the underwear in the garbage.

The next morning his body was swollen. When he stood, his left hip slipped from the socket before finding its new place a quarter inch left. Both ankles were loose. It hurt to put clothes on. He was scared to breath, and when he did, deciding on a big inhale to see just how bad it could be, the air flowed over something sharp.

Days later in the mine he found black crystals during a strong rainstorm and odd day of extreme heat, and desperate to heal, willing to try anything, he accepted a double-dog-dare from Bob T. and ate three chunks. He brainstormed ideas on count when his brain unfolded and folded and unfolded again, the feeling of black crystal in his body a new machine to revisit. He had no anger toward Dad, only fear, and thought of giving him, not Mom, a black crystal as a gift, an apology for being the type of kid who embarrassed his parents, who deserved to be punished for the way he was, what he did.

The pain from the punishment has stayed. He moves in ways so he doesn't feel it. For example, he knows not to lean too hard on his left hip. He forgets at moments, like playing basketball, when he drives the baseline and tries for a lay-up he's too far under to make. He takes a step under, to the far side of the rim, and his hip makes a loud *pop*, turning the guard's hamburger-head in the window. He launches three-pointers that force him to land hard on the heels of his feet. His foot throbs numbers.

He can't hit a shot. Everything bricks. When the ball gets trapped between rim and backboard the guard with the hamburger-head who has a belly like a bag of trash comes in and knocks it free by jumping with his club, his keys jangling and pants sagging. He grabs the ball and continues shooting, trying to hit the simplest of shots and misses each one.

With every missed shot his body hurts and he can smell his shit coming in through the vents in waves, crashing into the fans above who spin the shit and flatten-out the shit. Guards crowding by the window crawl over each other and laugh as he misses. He stands two feet from the hoop and raises the ball with one hand. *Push.* And miss. A muffled yell from a guard against bulletproof glass says, "Gotta be kidding me!"

It's my fault for hiding my underwear and it's my fault she's sick.

The steel white doors unlock and open, meaning the hour is up. He has one shot left. *Flick the wrist.* Swish.

Pants says, "I'm a winner," with his arms raised, ponytail a dog's tail, the ball rolling to a stop at the colored, padded wall. He thinks of Mom and the previous health meeting when he discussed the rape in the mine and how it dug up sadness, frustration, odd attraction, things no boy should witness or have to process. How he felt guilty for doing nothing. But now he has another chance. He will escape. He will see her again. He will find a way to add and make things better. He stops jumping, a sharp pain connecting his foot to his lower back.

When the guard with the hamburger-head puts a hand on his left shoulder Pants falls to his knees and grabs the guard's hand which goes limp. The guard reaches for his baton at his belt. The shit comes down from the ceiling and Pants vomits blue slush into his right hand and the guard says to him they need more crystal. Pants tells him to stop, there's little left, who are you, who is anyone.

A village myth says the sun will rage war on the earth. This is not a myth. Another village myth says the city will move into the village and crush it, that the city is alive, that it's a creature who eats the small. This too is not a myth. A third village myth says the black crystals are reaching up and pulling on the sun's flames, but no one knows for sure if that's true or not. Could just be a myth.

18

Ricky and Bobby T. take turns shoving each other into the fence. The chain-linked metal absorbs their bodies before springing them back. Coating half the sky, the sun. There's a theory that if you put a frog in water and raise the temperature half degree by half degree the frog won't notice, that the frog will stay in the water and die in the water. The Brothers walk and Ricky and Bobby T. continue shoving each other.

"You know what I hate," says Ricky. "Frogs."

"So?" says Bobby T.

Z. tells them to be quiet and they nod. He's trying not to act nervous, but this is the big day, this is the beginning of becoming remembered forever and his legs are shaking.

They total seven men dressed in khaki pants and powder-blue shirts. Z. is the exception. He wears black pants and a cream-colored button down. A dogtooth-shaped whistle on a string dangles around his neck. Green fabric torn from his grandfather's robe is tied around his left wrist.

"This is it," he says. "No turning back now."

Ricky moves the knife. With the help of Bobby T. they open the fence.

They stand at the bottom of the cliff. At the top is The Bend. Before they climb, everyone but Z. removes handcuffs from their pockets. Z. locks their wrists behind their backs. All eyes sting with sweat.

The sun boils clouds.

The sky bleached.

They follow Z. up the cliff. They fall and slide and claw and become covered in dirt, just how they planned. They climb with their heads down, blinking from the raining dirt. Ricky is a bit dramatic and falls several times on purpose, flopping back down the cliff with his legs outstretched. Dirt fills their shoes and dirt pours down their backs and dirt becomes stuck in their sweat. They find levels of harder dirt they use as stairs and they climb to the top. A few city gawkers holding binoculars step back and mumble. A young girl holds a phone into the sky and moves her thumb up and down against the screen. A man with a face like a horse says they look funny. He tries to say more but chokes on the candy he's eating. His wife slaps his back and he walks away, head down, one arm raised, swallowing.

They walk in a single file line with Z. leading and the sun following. After a half mile through the outskirts of the city, the Brothers looking into the streets and seeing things like dogs dressed in leather jackets, big suits on little men, hairy neck = gold chain, twenty types of bottled water, electronic shirts, traffic lights somersaulting green-yellow-red, neon signs, everything electric and somehow not powered by yellow crystals, everything big and ugly and loud, the intricate brickwork of the prison comes into focus.

"Everyone okay?" says Z.

If there was a problem someone would speak because the plan said so.

Z. walks painfully tall. He tells himself that he's in control because he's the kind of person who is never in control. He doesn't perspire much, but the heat pulsates against his ears. His heart beats scary fast so he relaxes with conscious rhythmic breathing (Pants wrote that city people do yoga and detailed something called Prana). He tells himself everything will be okay. The jailbreak in reverse will be his greatest accomplishment because it has to be.

"Good," he says. "Let's go."

They prepare their facial expressions as they reach the prison.

A glass booth shouldered by gates and barbed wire is the first encounter. Behind the gates and glass booth is a paved road to the prison entrance. There's a door, ADMINISTRATION, with two guards standing at either side. The guards are dressed like the guard inside the glass booth Z. makes eye contact with – perfectly pressed blue pants and crisp tucked-in blue shirts.

A drain in the glass booth, face level, holds a metal net that distorts his voice when he speaks into it, "Good morning. Reporting."

"What?" says the guard, a short man with blue eyes, head shaved and wrinkled with fat. There's a motorized fan clipped in the corner of the booth on full blast. It appears to do little to cool. He's the sweatiest person Z. has ever seen.

"Reporting," he repeats, the last few letters, the "ing," an embarrassing high pitch, Z. not totally positive if what he was told to say by Pants is right.

"Reporting?" says the guard who draws his gun from the holster. "Reporting what?"

Z. wonders if what he was told, what he remembered from the letters, has become scrambled in his head and he's getting it all wrong. But that's impossible. He's spent endless hours memorizing the plan nailed to his bedroom wall, highlighted with red pen.

"Exchange inmates from Willows Bay," he says looking at the Brothers. "Standard set here. Shouldn't take long. You believe this heat? The sun. Heck, I remember when I'd stand at The Bend and watch the turquoise sky and don't think we'll ever see that again. Nah, all different now."

"Right," says the guard.

His gun is halfway drawn. Z. looks like the typical transfer guard with necklace whistle and cream-colored shirt. There's a weird piece of green fabric at his wrist but that's nothing too strange because transfer guards are an odd bunch and there's such a high turnaround for the job. And the exchange inmates all have the facial expressions of men with nothing to do but think about what they are recently found guilty of. The guard studies them. Nods Z. up and down.

"They say we're not coming?" says Z. "Typical."

"I get mad," says the guard.

The Brothers, minus Z., take turns looking at the sky, their boots, everyone making tough-guy faces.

Just trust and follow the plan – Pants.

Inside the glass booth is a computer. The guard's fingers graze the letters QWERTY, his eyes narrowed and mean at Z. before he slaps the gun back into his holster. The noise makes Z. flinch and prepare to absorb a bullet. Then the guard says, "Ah, I'm messing with YOU. You need a blood transfusion? Look white. GOT YOU. Got you *real* good. Oh man did I get you good."

"R-r-r-reporting," repeats Z. This was never mentioned. "I'm just… reporting like I'm s-s-s-supposed to. Reporting."

The guard bounces inside the booth drum-slapping the walls. Then he starts patting his pockets. He's incredibly short – his height barely increases when he stands from the swivel stool and Z. notices a rectangular clip on his breast pocket engraved with his name, Karl.

"I do this all the time, newbie," says Karl. "Getting people is what I do." With a pen he pulls from his pants pocket he writes a single | in a notebook filled with pages of |.

Z.'s shoulders drop. He remembers his breathing. The air is disgusting. He composes himself back into character, remembers something Pants said in a previous letter and he laughs, shakes his head, slaps the glass twice and says, "Fucker, you did. Now open up before these boys die of heat stroke."

"Heat wave gonna kill us all," says Karl jingling a ring of keys. "But nobody wants to listen to me. Man, did I get you guys. Might be the best get I've ever gotten. Hold on."

Z. and the handcuffed Brothers mingling behind him stay on script. Some stand looking at their feet hiding their smiles, others are puffed-chest and tight-jawed. Ricky, on the verge of fake crying, rubs the side of his face against his shoulder. Karl comes of his booth and a buzzer goes off. He nods at Ricky and says to Z., "Always one in the bunch, huh."

"Yeah," says Z. "It's the guys who can shut themselves off who survive."

"You know the drill," says Karl.

The notes, the guidelines, the advice from the letters, are working. Even Z. is kind of surprised when they get access into the prison. Bobby T. smiles as the gates open to ringing bells and then he stops smiling when Z. gives him a real mean look. The bells sound like the days of worship when the mine workers announced green and red crystal finds. Bobby T. was a child running to the mine with dozens of kids, pushing and swerving around each other, never tripping. He held a big green one up to the sun and it looked like water.

The wind blows their shirts into fat suits. Bobby T., as instructed to do at various times, spits, and the saliva wraps around his cheek. He attempts to slap the spit from his beard but forgets the handcuffs and the hot metal digs into his wrists. He rolls a shoulder and the saliva comes off on his shirt in a solid leash.

"Pick up the pace," says Karl.

They follow, trying not to stare at Karl's height. Z. thinks about saying some city-speak, maybe ask him if there's ever been a population increase of midgets.

Splitting the guards, they walk through the open door and into an office where three women in white blouses with blond hair sit behind a marble counter. The women look up at the group entering with the rush of humid air. Before the door shuts one of the women gets a good look at the sky and her eyes widen. When the door shuts, her expression goes right back to before, a numb forever-lost look. Gray and blue cubicles cram the room, phones ring, and the tops of people's heads float above padded walls.

Z. takes a deep breath. "We made it," he says and immediately feels judged, scared, for saying out loud what he meant to think.

"No, you didn't," says a woman in white, searching with her hands over the empty desk. "We don't have a report for new inmates, or a transfer, or an exchange, or any paperwork at all."

"You're absolutely right, Toby," says another woman. "Looks like we have ourselves a problem."

Z. doesn't have a wrap for this situation because he was told by Pants that once inside there would definitely be paperwork and the Brothers would be moved into the appropriate cells. He wonders how many midgets live in the city and why they exist. He hears someone slam a phone down followed by the phone crashing against a wall. A man in a charcoal suit with spiked hair runs from one end of the room to the other waving a folder. The women in white smile at Karl whose cheeks are full of air as his blue eyes wobble. Half his head is above the counter. His body is shaking. One of the women leans over, rolls her eyes, and pokes his right cheek. His face farts.

"BAHAHAHAHA," says Karl, collapsing to the floor. "I get you again, and again, and again," he says, emphasizing each *again* with a mock windmill punch on the carpet. When he stands, he marks another | in his book. "Shit," he exhales. "I'm on fire."

"Sorry," says the woman sitting in the middle. "Little Karl is that kind of person. We agree, on occasion, to play along. Besides, it's all in good fun. Nobody gets hurt."

"What kind of person is he?" asks Z., smiling, maybe flirting with the woman because her face appears backlit by the sun. He's heard about this before via a city television commercial – lipstick, eye shadow, mascara, and bronzer. She makes him smile like a dope, yes, fun fun. Or maybe he smiles because smiling, he was told by Pants, makes city people give you what you want.

"An asshole," says the woman to the right. "That's what kind of person he is."

"Go in and I'll pass this upstairs and these guys here will be set and good to go and they can move on with their lives and – " says the woman in the middle, saying the words so familiar they kind of bleed together, a script she's said ten thousand times before. She trails off and her face is expressionless, dimming. "What was I saying?"

"Had my fun for the day," says Little Karl. "Jug will finish the transfer up. Nice meeting you." Little Karl walks out the door, says, "See ya later, fellas," to the guards, waves his book at them, and re-enters the glass booth with the computer and corner fan which he holds his hand near to see if it's working.

"Seriously," repeats the woman, "What was I talking about? Toby?"

The Brothers move from the administrative office and through a seven-foot-high security turnstile and into the second floor of the prison – a place of blue metal, skylights, concrete floors, everything built in hard steel lines. People are yelling and hitting things made out of metal onto things made of metal and there are shadows where there shouldn't be shadows. The prison is huge but it feels small and cramped to the Brothers, every hallway and turn is like navigating a closet in extreme heat with no ventilation.

"This way."

Following Jugba Marzan, inmates size up the Brothers as they walk a kind of open hallway with cells on the right side, a net on the left side. Below the net, and a good fifty feet down, an open concrete center with patrolling guards, more cells. Z. looks back and shrugs. The light in the prison fades with passing clouds. Jug walks in slow motion. His khaki pants are worn high, his backside large and lumbering and dimpled with sweat.

A man with a square head with hair like a bed of needles takes a plank of wood, a section of his bedframe, and thrusts it between the bars, stabbing Ricky in the shoulder who falls into the net attached between the ceiling and the metal railing. When the net tears, two guards catch him and pull him back. Inmates cheer.

The Brothers forget everything they've learned. This wasn't supposed to happen, maybe it's another game by Karl, but no, this is different, this is pure violence, and Z. rescans all the letters, and the plan, the red underlines all over his bedroom walls and comes up with nothing.

Z., breaking out in a full body sweat, overwhelmed with what he's gotten himself into, the prison a place of terror, nothing like the pamphlet leads one to believe, taps Jug on the shoulder and says the paper specifies what inmates he's taking.

"I know," says Jug.

"McDonovan," says Z. standing on his toes, aiming his words over Jug's shoulder. "The Sky Father Gang."

"I'm a counselor, well, a supervisor, so I understand people. We have these health meetings. I've learned things. I know what you're telling me. Hey, I get it."

Z. looks behind him and everyone is gone except Bobby T. who is on his knees and surrounded by guards holding batons high. One of the guards is wearing a giant gold cross and telling Bobby T. to pray, instructing him how to properly bend forward, where to place his hands on the floor which the guard guides with little kicks. Bobby T. keeps pulling his hands back toward himself because he's being kicked. One baton moves.

"Jailbreak in reverse," says Jug.

"What?" says Z.

"Amazing."

Z. is covered in sweat and his clothes feel heavy, like they are pulling him to the ground. His legs are sore with the panic settling into his flesh. He wipes his forehead with the torn piece of green robe tied to his wrist and his hair is soaked. He pulls the sleeve of his shirt back over the piece of green fabric. He's not sure what to say. He's not sure what to do. What would The Sky Father Gang do. What would his grandfather do. What would anyone who doesn't want to die do.

"Karl put you up to this? Keeps getting us." Then village Z. coming out, the man who once jumped from a table in the street to a moving truck's hood: "I'm leaving."

"No joke," Jug says, who opens an empty cell.

Z. considers running. Guards approach from either end of the hallway. More inmates cheering and bells going off and guards telling inmates to be quiet because there's nothing to see. Sharpened spoons flung from cells. When Z. gets a good look of the prison from where he stands all he sees are dark boxes with bars, stacked side by side and on top of each other. A guard is picking up the spoons as more spoons are thrown.

"Come in," says Jug. "I need to ask you a favor. You don't know it now, but this will work out for the best, for both of us."

Inside the cell Jug appears fatter. His face is doughy and his neck is red from shaving. He has the general appearance of a man once in good shape and in control of his life, in Younger Years, but is now someone uncomfortable with the body he's in. He moves as if he doesn't fully understand it. He hates the size of his shirts. When he showers, he stares not at the size of his dick, but his stomach.

"Black crystal," says Jug, sitting down on the cot. "We're addicted."

"My job is to bring them in," says Z., going back on script, still trying to pull off the impossible. He knows a black crystal doesn't exist, so what Jug says about it doesn't register. He moves back and forth from terror to strength and back again.

"You guys acting like kids, smearing shit on your faces to mess with others, putting a table in the middle of the road, I mean."

"What?"

A guard locks the door. The clang raises Z.'s shoulders.

"Basketball accident," says Jug wincing, reaching for his ankle to tie his shoe. "We have a court here. Half a court. Was going in hard when Little Karl, who will be happy to know can mark up his book when I'm done here, decides to take a charge. I sort of pulled back," Jug leans backward with his right arm swan shaped, "and pulled off this beauty of a one-hand floater. That didn't stop my body from toppling over into Little Karl. Damn, it hurt. Never felt pain like that before, like my whole body was shook-up inside. I didn't make the shot."

Z. backs up against the cell bars, cold. He's four feet from where Jug sits but it feels like inches. He breaths in the prison and listens to the ugly sounds from within it.

"I," says Z. "T-t-t-this place – "

Sweat and urine and men kept in vomit-filled boxes they decorated but are never cleaned have been molded in the heat for weeks. The prison isn't like Z. was told. The prison isn't like how it's promoted to everyone outside it. The prison is a place worse than any part of the village. And since the heat wave was noticeable, since the black crystal has been depleting and getting scary low, things have only gotten worse.

"When it gets hot in here, right at peak late afternoon heat, it smells like a pig farted through a cigarette," says Jug. "Is that an image or what?" Jug smiles way longer than anyone should smile after saying something so disgusting and then gets serious, smoothing the chest of his shirt, the professional version of himself coming on. "And every few months a group not totally unlike yourselves tries to rescue someone. Usually over-eager city folk with some messed up relative the system got wrong, should have been placed in Willows Bay, right. But everyone likes it here. Okay, not everyone, I see the way you're looking at me, but why leave something that takes care of you? For example, you could have the worst mom in the world who brings home retards, but she feeds you chicken and buys you jeans and washes your bedsheets, and you forget how she yells and screams and drinks too much and makes the retards breakfast in the morning while they sit slumped, but not you, you don't say a word because you have it easy with a mom like that, you're taken care of and you don't leave it."

Z. senses bodies behind him. He's lean and muscular, sure, a little belly on him, and he's always prided himself that he can take care of himself in a fight, but now, he's terrified.

"There's been a mistake," he says. "You said something about black crystal."

"It's tricky to reseal an envelope and not have the receiver be suspicious. What you do is use steam from an iron," says Jug, and he runs an imaginary iron over his thigh.

Through the bars a hairy hand massages the back of his neck and Z. tries to walk forward and the hand squeezes. A hush of male voices blends with the concrete echoes and metallic sounds of the prison. Z. imagines crawling through the crystal mine dirt as a child, licking it, then getting yelled at by Mom, her hand gripping his neck.

"You don't want to see what's behind you," says Jug. "I figured you'd want to free him. He's a good one. That black crystal does all sorts of stuff. Makes you feel superman. Problem is we're about to run out. That's why I wanted to talk to you, that's why I let you in here in the first place. All this is going to turn out for the better, you'll see."

"It's a m-m-m-myth," says Z.

"I'm afraid, good sir," says Jug, so confident now, not like the previous health meeting, "that you're incorrect."

"It's just dark-colored red," says Z. "You're living a lie."

"Not sure that matters because really, we're running out,"

says Jug. He reaches his hand into a pants pocket and scratches himself.

"Then walk in and steal some. Send Mob of Mary's."

Inmates cheer in a rhythmic sing-song way and Z. wonders what's happening. Is Bobby T. dead? The prison is evil. Arnold is probably saying something offensive. His arms will be torn off by dogs.

"I've read the letters. You're smart," says Jug, "and also dumb. My sister is like this. She's the smartest dumb person I know. She has two college degrees and when we get together with Mom she always makes the last point, always breaks people down. She's unemployed and has never held a job for longer than a month she's so smart."

"I remember looking for them," says Z. "Everyone digging around like crazy in the rain because someone said they thought they saw one."

From his pocket where his hand scratched, Jug pulls out a tiny twisted branch of black crystal. He holds it up in the dull light between his thumb and finger, turning it and rolling it between his fingers. It's about two inches long and in its thinness looks breakable. The blackness is undeniable, and without realizing what he's doing, Z. reaches out to touch it and the hand on his neck digs in deeper and pulls him back. In the jerking-back-to-reality motion Z. thinks the crystal has to be a fake, a set-up, no way, how is it possible.

"They exist," says Jug, carefully placing the black crystal back in his pocket. "It's very simple what I'm asking here. No bullshit."

Z. says it's just a dark-colored red, you're being fooled, total bullshit. *Everyone is eventually fooled into believing in something that doesn't exist. Give meaning to your existence no matter what.* Z. remembers this passage from one of the books, and he's proud of himself for being able to recite it, it seems so powerful, it sounds so good, but it has no effect whatsoever on Jug who just sits with a neutral facial expression. And the more Z. thinks about it, the more he thinks maybe it is a black. He too wants to believe.

"You're perfect because you live there. Spending time in the mine won't be odd compared to, you know, Mob of Mary's, or someone from here going in that deep."

"It does something to your insides?"

"Yes," says Jug, kind of looking at Z. with a half smirk and general disbelief. "You're not like my sister, no, not at all. You have things at stake and you'll work hard to make sure everything works out."

"It's not supposed to happen like this. This place, in here, isn't like how people think it is."

"If one exists," says Jug, "more exist."

Z. getting anxious and self-conscious: "H-h-h-how am I s-s-s-suppose to f-f-f-feel about this?"

"Feel good."

Z. races back through memories of Younger Years but can't find a black crystal. Generations have looked and failed. Some believe that a combination of rain and heat bring them up, but this has never been proven, only rumored. It will be impossible to find in hours, days, what has been worked at for years. Z. feels lightheaded, like he might pass out with the next breath. Everything – the heat, the sun, the stress of the jailbreak in reverse, what his life is or isn't – is killing him. He imagines his count as salt in a half circle around his boots.

There's a long pause. More bells ringing. Someone from the second floor throws a shoe filled with rocks at a window. Jug shakes his head, rubs his face with two sweaty hands. "Go into the mine and bring back more black crystal. That's it."

Z.'s shoulders feel like they are arching around his head. The hand is still on him. "I don't think I can do that."

"We don't trust anyone here."

"I think we should just forget all this."

Prison noise and silence in the cell, Jug just staring through Z.

"I could list everything that would happen to your friends," says Jug. "Listen, I've read the letters multiple times, they're fascinating. You want to be someone important, that's fine, I understand that urge. But it's greed. Don't pretend it's something more or something different. I'm here to help though, because my greed is black crystal and being the guy who gets it. Bring it back here and you'll be remembered, that's what you want, I know that and you know that. Win-win. See?"

Another hand from behind runs up the inside of Z.'s leg.

"But what you're asking me to do is impossible," says Z. "This feels like a t-t-t-trick."

"What you'll learn," says Jug, "is that everything is a trick. Only thing that isn't is the universe. I'm talking about outer space, the sun, the moon, planets, stuff we don't know about. No humor out there. Serious business among those stars. The universe does whatever it wants while we're forced to play games. We've all thought about our lives compared to what's above, right? Think about it, the universe is going to live forever. No counting days or crystals. No last breaths with loved ones. The universe will just keep expanding. Do you understand what I'm saying? It's important that we just do what it is we do and we keep doing it for as long as possible."

Z. imagines an entire network of black crystals underground. It has to be a fantasy. But he saw it, Jug held it up for that quick moment, and he's never seen a crystal like that before. Was it just a red, this messed jail lighting, his exhaustion, his mind dimming the color? Why would someone like Jug make up such a story if it wasn't real?

"What I'm saying is, you had your own idea of a game to keep you occupied. A jailbreak in reverse. I mean, *fuck*, stupid and somehow brilliant. That's why you can do this. And we have a game in here where guards take black crystal, and when they don't they act like idiots. They hurt more. What are we suppose to do – fire them and let them tell the media what's going on?

PR disaster. I feel like I'm talking to myself here. This is the game we want to keep playing and there isn't anything wrong with that. The game is what keeps you distracted from the universe bearing down on you."

"I understand," says Z., "but I don't know what's happening."

"I'll give you a few days. I'm not sure your friends can last more. Come back with it and they walk. Pants too. As a matter of fact, all the villagers in here, everyone goes, why not. You'll be remembered as the man who sprung your people free. They'll build you a statue and you'll be remembered forever. Don't let me keep you longer. The guards get wild without it. No telling what they might do to your friends while you're away. And no telling what they may do if we can't control them, maybe run rabid to his home and find the one his mom has in that box. Only so much I can do here. Come on, let's go."

Z. runs under the sun-clogged sky. He makes eye contact with a man wearing a dress sitting on the stoop of a brick building. The man raises his arm slowly, the sleeve of his blue dress gathering around his elbow, and while coughing, he gives Z. the middle finger. Z. runs faster. He puts the city on his back. The man holds his middle finger as high as his arm will stretch, leans forward in the direction of Z. who slides down the cliff, creating long dusty tunnels in the air above.

17

The sky is laced with turquoise worms, and where the sun normally is there's two red lips, a parting mouth with clouds for teeth. Her bed contains 24 stacked pillows that form a wall. She gets into bed and looks up at the black crystal drawn on the ceiling. She closes her eyes, steadies her breathing, and touches the pillows. The mouth in the sky fills with red and the teeth vanish and it's the sun. The worms wail and turquoise cascades down an arc in the sky.

The first pillow Remy places on her feet. The next, her legs. The next, her stomach. Finally, her chest. She builds layers until she has to balance the pillows on her body with her breathing. She puts the last three pillows on her head and hugs her face until she passes out. Her arms flop off the sides of the bed and her fingertips dangle near the floor.

She's a baby. She takes wide, unsteady steps, and on a few occasions, tips backward, arms extended as her diaper thumps the floor. She wears a blue shirt with a hand-drawn black crystal (Brother). Her face is blond hair. She stumbles from her bedroom and into the hallway where she falls down the stairs, blond hair blown open and her body awkwardly sliding down the stairs as Mom shouts from below. Afterward, Remy cried for fourteen hours. Mom stayed awake the entire time, tapping her back in sets of ten, feeding her sips of tea, telling her it would be okay, they will come back on again.

Remy twitches in the wobbly picture and her eyelids flicker. Her arm as baby arm snaps like a bird's spine beneath a boot. The pillows fall. One hits her arm. Mom moans from her bedroom. Her negative weight floats upward from her refusal of food. Her falling numbers hurt everything around her, even the carpet looks depressed. Dad skips between loving companion to distant husband to angry father. He spends his days alone. Each day this week he's been sitting gargoyle-perched on the roof. Recently, Remy's thought the problem of Mom's sickness isn't Mom's sickness exactly, but Dad's reaction to Mom's sickness.

Remy writes in a notebook:

FELL DOWNSTAIRS AS A BABY -5 CRYSTALS.

SUBTRACT -1 FOR EVERY YEAR AFTER FROM AGING.

She puts three pillows on her face and grips tight until she passes out again, her hands falling off the bed, eyes now moving over a dark road. She's riding her bike with the blue and yellow tassels tied to the handlebar. She wanted red and green, to be special, but Dad bought the commons. This vision like the last is broken from reality but more severe – Remy riding her bike on the road to the mine, blue and yellow tassels blowing endlessly backward and touching her home. Her hair is also endlessly long and it touches the house. She's followed by a spotlight. Her feet blur on the pedals. She's trying to escape the light. Skin three inches above her right ankle catches on the rear derailleur and the bike breaks into a severe slide. Water sprays from where the tires skid. The road becomes a beach and Brother is standing there covered in glistening sweat, jogging in place, with Harvak at his side who is also jogging in place. Sea crystals the shape of hexagons colored white foam then harden to black stone on the sand. An octopus is flung by the sun across the sky. The spotlight disappears and the man, who looks just like Dad, who held the spotlight, twirls his hand goodbye, bows, then jumps off the cliff at the top of The Bend.

-8 CRYSTALS FROM BIKE ACCIDENT.

She creeps down the staircase and sees only legs in the kitchen. She can't understand how they can stand so close to each other and yell so loud, how can their faces not split and bruise. Mom is doing almost all the shouting and her legs are following Dad's legs around the kitchen. He's cooking something and trying to avoid her. The thrill of watching her parents in this raw, private moment makes Remy's heart race and hands grip the wooden banister. They have always been so troubled, so doomed. They have always talked around each other. The pillows tumble again and the black crystal drawing on her ceiling comes into focus.

-4 CRYSTALS FROM DAMAGING PARENTS' WORDS ENTERING MY BRAIN.

She continues the game until her skin turns blue and she needs a tiny black crystal flint to regain strength. She stabs her mouth. A freckle expands through her cheek in a red circle that covers one side of her face. The following visions of all things negative she sees awake: Harvak dying, Brother leaving, parents fighting, sun killing. Then, there's the beach again and the clouds are slowly coming down and each one holds a cop holding a baby under an arbor rung with flowers.

Black crystal dissolves everything.

Black crystal is everything.

Here she is with limbs shaking, lungs sky-up and filling with the good kind of pain, head all air, Remy with eyes glazed-over and wanting everyone she loves to live forever.

+25 FROM BLACK CRYSTAL.

"Mom, I need to speak to you, Mom," she says, knocking on the door and not waiting for an answer, flinging open the door and walking into the bedroom where Mom sits on the floor in a hunched lotus position. Her spine is visible through her night-gown (Chapter 4, Death Movement, Book 8) in the sunlight coming in through the window. When she turns and sees Remy, she slides a red box under the bed.

"What's wrong?"

"I ran the mine during the rainstorm. I know, I know, I shouldn't, but I did, and it happened."

"You're sick?"

"With Hundred. A truck almost ran us over. I have to tell you something."

"I saw the mud. Come here."

Remy sits in the folded angles of Mom's lap and it's the first time she thinks maybe she's too big for this, but being so close to Mom is comforting, even in the heat. She places her head on Mom's chest and there's no heartbeat. Wait. There it is.

"Black crystals," says Remy, looking up at Mom's chin. "They exist. They cut my feet and I felt a rush. I know, it's wrong. But Mom, I'm sorry. I've done it again and I'm telling you it adds. I have some left and I don't think there's more left in the whole world."

Mom moves Remy's head and body facing forward toward the window so Remy can't see her skin. Last night, Dad found red scabs in the shape of a door on the back of her neck. "Your Brother talked about this."

She couldn't remember the last time Mom said the word *Brother* or his real name, Adam. Remy never saw him use black

63

crystal for sure, but she assumed he had it. There was a night when she walked past his bedroom and he was in there with three kids and they were taking turns eating a dark-colored rock. Brother used one side of his mouth to gnaw on it while the others jumped on the bed and told him to keep going, eat it all. It was a dare. Then he acted funny. He ran in place and dripped sweat and slapped his face. He fell to the floor and barked. He rolled over and looked up at Remy and screamed to close the door. After one of the boys slammed it closed they laughed forever. They ran and threw their bodies against the door and she could see little slivers of light around the doorframe and she stepped back thinking the little slivers of light were forming a box around her.

"It could help you. Or what about the hospital?"

"You're still doing it? You have some left?"

The lace curtains pulled open are singed black at the edges.

"No," lies Remy. She can still feel the black crystal inside her. Her feet keep moving when she doesn't want them to move.

"Remy."

"Just try?"

"Do you have any left?"

"I said no."

Mom rubs Remy's shoulders. "Children replace their parents."

Remy stands, her legs momentarily tangled inside of Mom, and stomps her feet. She marches. Mom pushes herself backward trying to avoid getting crushed. Remy's face is all knots, and her cheek, where she placed the black crystal flint, is swollen. She gives one more monster stomp and the sunlight triangle shakes.

A fire truck's siren can be heard in the distance and they both look at the window. More city buildings are burning, flames mending seamlessly with sunlight.

Mom looks up at Remy, a shifting adult-to-child perspective that saddens Mom. "This is what happens."

Remy asks, "How many?"

"It's something you don't need to know."

"Tell me."

"No."

"I'll feel better knowing what's inside you."

"Remy, please."

"But how many? If I have to accept it, I should know it. Mom? Please?"

"Two."

16

He sits on the roof in the midnight dark. New lights shine from the city. Buildings built in hours. One building shoots up so fast that Dad closes one eye and with his opposite hand finger-walks the sky with each level completed. Windows with workers' flashlights open to his touch. The sound of hammers fold inside the sound of saws.

City inspectors are told to sleep outside and report back to Sanders if the city is growing. The inspectors wear white helmets with flashlights and one-piece jumpers the color of pearl. At night they patrol the fence with their lights crisscrossing as they examine the ground. They measure the dirt between the fence and the nearest buildings, and each time the measurement shrinks a quarter-inch.

"What's going on?" says one inspector to another, in a concrete stairwell that rises with each word spoken. "We losing our minds from the heat?"

"Beats me."

"We have to report something, Jim."

"I told you, it beats me."

"What does that mean?"

"Means I don't know."

"How can we not know?"

"Just don't."

Later: "Well," says Sanders, who is aging quickly, not the young buck who once gave a speech at the opening of the prison. He's balding. In his closet in his office, worn under a suit jacket and pressed between two suits, is a blue dress. Only his wife knows about this fetish, and one day soon, his son.

The ten dirt-encrusted inspectors stand in the room and their jumpsuits crinkle with movement. Sanders stares. One inspector has his flashlight on. Another inspector pulls the helmet off his head and with the heel of his palm knocks the batteries out and onto the floor. They do their best to stand silent.

"We don't know why, or how," says an inspector. "Also, the sun might be getting closer, but our reports say it's an optical illusion."

"And how, exactly, is that supposed to make sense?" says Sanders.

"What? The sun, or the city? Or both?"

"Let's start with the city."

"It doesn't," says the same inspector. His black mustache is saturated with sweat. "It doesn't make any sense at all, that's what we're trying to tell you. Not sure if the land is retracting or these buildings are new buildings. I know what that sounds like. We orange-tag them and the tags disappear. Is someone, maybe a villager, taking the tags off? I doubt it. Could be the guy who keeps lighting our buildings on fire. What I'm saying is that one of us sleeps in a building only to wake up with a building in front of that building."

"Ghosts are working the night shift?" asks Sanders.

The inspector without a helmet says, "I touched the sky where the sun is and burned my fingers."

"No, well, not exactly," says the sweaty black mustache. "We can't prove that. We can't prove that because we have no physical proof of seeing the buildings going up. Yes, we see, we understand, there is less land between the village and here. Yes, there seems to be more random buildings, but, I, we, just don't know."

"Did you ever think," says Sanders, rubbing his face with both hands, "to have one, maybe two people, stay up for a few days and just watch, or, I don't know, take a few pictures? We have so much technology, use it."

"But we did," says the sweaty black mustache. "And we didn't see anything. There's no proof of construction, only what our eyes see, which is new buildings, fully constructed."

"That sounds," says Sanders, "insane."

"We know."

"Last question," says Sanders, sighing and looking frustrated at a maroon-draped window. He wants to take over the village, he wants it more than anything, but he also wants to control it, to understand it. He has speeches to give. He has an election to win. "In your inspectors' opinions, is the city, however impossible that it can grow on its own accord, actually *growing*?"

The sweaty black mustache takes a deep breath and his protective suit crinkles. "Yes," he exhales.

Half of Dad's body hangs over the edge of the roof. He asks a group of nightwalkers below dressed in dark robes with droopy hoods if they've noticed the city changing shape. Dad wonders if they're Black Mask, the ones burning the buildings.

With faces turned up they whisper-yell, "OF COURSE WE HAVE YOU FOOL FACE. THEY WILL MOVE RIGHT IN. HA! HA! HA! DID YOU HEAR US? WE SAID, HA! HA! HA!"

"Are you Black Mask?"

"NO!"

"Are you sure?"

"POSITIVE!"

The air is so hot he doesn't want to breath. He lies back on the roof, studies the sky, and sees a woman in a constellation whose elbows are stars. Circling his finger he spins a crystal balanced on her lips. He whispers her name. He wants to cry, the idea is there, but he doesn't because his emotions kept inside have cemented him, have hurt him over the years, and to let it out now would be impossible. He imagines his count attacked with sun-red knives. But whatever he's at is nothing compared to Mom because she could be at one. She could be an ant. She could be a flower. He didn't help her. Dad doesn't have relationships, he has obligations, like making dinner and keeping the generator going. He spins the crystal until it burns a hole through her mouth.

When he stops spinning she vanishes and white lines that connected stars, created legs, arms, her face, become birds, rats, deer. He thinks he sees a rabbit, her favorite animal, fall from the sky and land on the roof of a building being set on fire by a man without a shirt.

I need sleep, I'm losing it, help me.

Below him his family is trying to sleep. He imagines the house is transparent, a dollhouse, and he's a hand crawling the floors, pulling a blanket to Remy's chin, moving the hair from his wife's eyes. He moves into the city, glides over the prison where his son sits on the roof… just… like… him… and Dad's hand pats him on the back then tugs his ponytail.

Standing on the roof, Dad admires the homes that are falling apart. Through a home's window, he sees water pouring from the ceiling. An old woman holds a bucket in her right hand and with her other hand she shakes her fist at the water. Skip Callahan runs into the room waving his arms, telling the woman to get away, he's here, he can help. He stands under the water with arms raised and the water gets stronger. He keeps screaming that he wants to help, he's a born helper, until the old woman pushes him out of the way with surprising force, nearly knocking Skip to the floor. She fills the bucket and signals him to get another. Dad looks back up at the buildings then back down and over the shacks.

As a child what you see is creation. As an adult what you see is destruction.

Dad leaves the roof by jumping into a pile of hay built in the backyard for such a stunt. One of the nightwalkers jerks his head around and whisper-yells, "BIRD MAN, CAREFUL, YOU'RE GOING TO HURT YOURSELF."

15

I'm going to bed," says Mom.

Remy reaches for words with her arms. When Mom peeks her head further into the room and sees her lying on her back in bed, knitting the air with her hands, Mom thinks Remy's dreaming so she closes the door.

Remy's taken the remainder of the found black crystals by tongue cutting. She hoped the black crystal contained powers. Total desperation to try and reverse what's always lowering. Remy scared and failing to save Mom. Ingesting black crystal is an effect similar to a flooding of poisonous berries in the bloodstream. But it does make you feel better, so she should just take it. Why should she watch Mom be pulled from her life without trying the one thing that contains movement? Most people are content to be squashed by city and sun. *Like Dad.*

Remy falls asleep and sees herself as a toddler. She's recently learned how to walk and Brother is running circles around her. They're playing spit-tag in the crystal mine. Brother runs, shouts, "You got crystal fungus ON YOUR FACE. IT'S ON YOU," and she can't keep up. Her spit is drool and bubble. Most kids would cry, but Remy laughs, she loves any game played with him, and she slaps her arms in the air as her spit and his spit mix on her face. Even when he rides his bike right in front of her, lands a glob across her eyes, she giggles, stomps her feet, and tries to open her eyes by blinking through the froth. The idea to run after him results in her falling.

When she wakes she asks for Mom to come back, she wants to say goodnight, she wants to say sorry for acting the way she did before. What does it feel like to have two left?

The black crystal drawing on the ceiling tells her in flashes of light that Mom will be taken. She understands the cruelty of the universe. She doesn't move and she doesn't speak. The black crystal inside her dissolves and cleans her blood black. She feels so alone. There's never anyone to talk to even when there's someone to talk to. You put your words onto a body and hope for an equal return. Tonight she'll stand naked at the bathroom mirror, and touching her stomach, wonder what's left.

14

A guard wearing a gold cross on a gold necklace picks at the donuts. One leans back to admire, he's actually smiling, the flow of coffee into his cup. Another sits on an invisible chair, his back against the wall, his face pained. His hands are on his thighs and every few seconds he adjusts his body, rubbing his ass against the wall, until he falls and the guard from the table touching all the donuts says, "You owe me ten."

Voices echo off metal and concrete. The door opens and then closes.

"Are you lazy now?" says Jug, sitting in a chair, legs spread wide, his torso leaning to the left, finger running back and forth between ankle and knee. "Used to iron in these creases so sharp I'd get goose-bumps. Seriously, goose-bumps."

When Pants rolls his neck he can't feel his head. His teeth hurt. His hair is uncombed and filthy, a hard mat of blond that has grown to the middle of his back. He still requests the top shaved and the look is disarming and absurd and the inmates aren't sure what to think but most decide to stay away.

"I'm doing the same job I've always done," Pants says, entering the circle of chairs.

The guards at the table take notice except the one on the floor fingering through his wallet.

"Sit," says Jug.

Pants pulls a chair away from the others, as far away as possible without being told to move closer.

"What," says Pants, sitting down, smiling, looking around the room. "This about laundry, really? I'll be more aware. I'll double check, but, you have to give me a break because, I'm just going through some stuff right now."

"You have it easy here," says Jug. "Everyone does. You do what you want, have a nice room – "

"Are told when to eat, sleep, shower, exercise. It's not like before. It's not like the beginning when we decorated our cells. What happened? Power and corruption. City values. This place is rotting from the inside. A guard told me there's moldy streaks running down the outside walls."

Jug smiles. In a way, he respects him for being disrespectful, and what Pants says is true. "Okay, some structure. A prison is a place to hold people who didn't follow the law and to help those people recover. The word is re-ha-bil-i-ta-tion. Nothing wrong with that I don't think. The way I see it, I'm part of helping people. Hey, you feeling all right?"

Pants hasn't had crystal in days. Besides, he's leaving this place soon. He's heard a rumor about the failure of the jailbreak in reverse, that some of the men are now in the prison for good. But he hasn't seen anyone and his closest gossipers – Tony and Pete – haven't said anything. He scratches his head and the sound is amplified and migraine producing. His forearms have blue-black veins like tangled wires. He imagines his count – 74, 55, 39, 28, 16, 10 – as actual numbers, three dimensional, falling in rain.

"Mom?"

Jug looks around the room and so does a guard. "Huh?" says Jug, leaning forward. From where Pants is sitting, combined with how Jug is sitting, Jug is two spread legs and just a head, a confused face in the middle, and Pants smiles, looks haunted.

"I don't want to do this anymore."

"I've had enough too. Got in a lot of trouble for what you did before. What I want to tell you is that we read your letters from Brothers Feast and the ones to and from your mother."

It's hard to say who is more shocked by his reaction – the guards who have their hands on their clubs, their fingers tracing the metal rings in the wood, or Pants himself, who feels the few muscles left in his body tighten like anchored rope. Even Jug is uncomfortable, his eyes zigzagging around the room as he ignores Pants who is crying the type of crying where the eyes are bloodshot and filled with water and the upper body shakes.

"Here's what's going to happen," says Jug, regaining his role as the one in control, his voice getting deep and serious, professional Jug acting quickly now, the guards wondering how he's going to handle this situation (a man crying!) after the last health meeting mishap. "Your friend will bring back the crystal or you're never going to leave this prison, never going to see your mom, never going to do a *thing*. Do you understand what I'm saying, a *thing*." He leans back and sneers, then leans forward again. The guards smile at each other and one tries to hold back his laughter by biting his bottom lip but exhales an odd half-hiss half-fart sound.

"I can't control what he does and doesn't do. If he comes back with it?"

"Everyone released," says Jug, proud of himself, relaxing back into the chair with his arms crossed over his chest. He's been able to handle Z. and the Brothers and now Pants. He's on top. He's in control. "Your poor mom."

Pants stands and jumps up on his chair. He grabs the back for balance before standing tall, arms outward.

"Hey," says Jug.

Everyone watches, not moving, not sure what to do.

Shuffling his feet, Pants turns so his back faces the guards. The plastic seat of the chair blows a bubble at the floor. He says he's going to fall backward. "Your choice to catch me."

Jug looks at the guards and shakes his head no.

But from instinct, maybe it was the trust-fall they did months ago, the guards begin to form two lines behind Pants. They disband when Jug says to them, "Stop, stop it. We can't let him tell us what to do. We're the ones in control."

Pants says to the wall, his feet a little shaky on the small surface of the chair, "Mom is slush."

The guard wearing the gold cross, which looks tiny now, says to another guard that it's because Pants doesn't believe in god, that's the reason he's unable to get over his guilt with what happened to his mother in the mine and the other guard says, "Frank, just stop."

"Better make your move, boss man," says Pants, and he pushes back on his heels.

Everyone watches as his weight shifts into the empty space of the room and into the odd frozen picture of a man tilting in the air, the body long, towering, insane.

The chair slides.

The guards have to react even if the reaction is not reacting.

Maybe you gain control by losing control.

The guard with the gold cross runs to the opposite wall and palm-punches a red button.

Maybe you're never in control and knowing that is gaining control.

"Shit," says a guard.

The chair hits the concrete wall, bounces backward and upward, spins and falls as Pants floats horizontal in the air. His face is flat and serene. His eyes are closed and all he sees is the blurry rose-tint of his eyelids, imagining the lights above are the sun.

Alarm bells ringing.

Guards running.

Jug shouts garbled letters. The power of his voice is one hand on each guard's shoulder, pulling them away from the body about to hit the concrete floor. They aren't prepared for the landing. They aren't prepared for the clean-up. What's about to happen is a horror, a body meeting an unmovable object, and it isn't the sound when his head cracks which is so horrendous, it's their voices.

13

Z. crawls under the fence. The air itself looks red, the wind a punishing speed, everything dusty, villagers walking in bent-over forward angles with eyes shut, hands as fists. There's a howling. The sun is trying to burn everything up and the buildings are moving closer. Returning took Z. a shorter amount of time than reaching the prison. Dirt fills his eyes but he doesn't care. He runs by a destroyed table and a crashed truck with flat tires. The tin roofs are blinding in the sun.

Everyone moves around the truck and table. Street vendors sell yellow crystal earrings, blue crystal necklaces, and green crystal headbands to a group of city tourists who have snuck in. There's a gold pin with a red crystal triangle inside. Drawings of what a black crystal would look like are also for purchase. Someone points at an old woman who kisses a green crystal she wears around her neck. They look at the village and think it's disposable, undesirable in modern time, something that can be washed away, or better, fixed. Z. moves past it all with the warning words of Jug ringing his head.

He runs to the mine dodging trucks. He jogs down the spiraling road. He passes little pyramids of dirt and mounds of yellow to be melted. Air conditioners from Mob of Mary's have been running on max, dripping gray water, trembling in too-large windows, poorly secured by old wadded up blankets. He runs unnoticed into a tunnel.

He scratches at the tunnel walls in random places and dirt and rocks rain on his shoes. He picks at silver flakes in the dark, truck headlights crossing him. He's been in the mine before, but not like this, not as a worker trying to find the impossible. He remembers the crystal Jug held and he still can't believe it because he's lived through the myth. No one, absolutely no one, has seen one up close. He has to discover something that doesn't exist. His mind buzzes, collapses, races. In the near distance the screech of a drill the size of the moon is terrifying, is some kind of machine at the edge of the city, is some kind of machine designed to build buildings impossibly fast. He saw them shooting up from the soil. He saw them moving closer. A man in a dress gave him the middle finger, what does that mean. They will bury the village in drywall, coffee shops, and wifi. He pulls off the dogtooth whistle and throws it behind him. They will bury the village in their future. He claws his hands into the wall of dirt and uses the weight of his body to drag his nails down until he lands on his knees. The city gets what it wants but so does the sun and one will destroy the other. He twists and turns his fist into the dirt until his knuckles tear.

Another chance to be remembered.

He digs until he can't feel his body, just the pain of dirt and rock beneath his fingernails. He digs until he believes, because he has to, that he can find a black crystal with no rain.

12

A wet cloth is placed on her forehead and is warm within seconds. Remy feeds her a teaspoon of broken black crystal in applesauce, the black particles tweezed from the fabric of her bedroom rug. The applesauce and crystals mix with Mom's saliva into a grim slush that glistens down her chin. Mom's acting like Harvak did.

"We'll check on you," Dad says. "Sleep."

When the door closes Mom throws her pillows to the floor, over the right side of the bed, and her body follows.

Reaching under the bed she grabs the red box. She drags herself across the floor, her legs motionless dead things, and into the sunlight triangle. She takes out the black crystal. Her hands have white veins, they look deep and faraway, drained. Little specks of flickering light swim through them. She angles the black crystal into the sun, and refracted high above and connected by thin bridges of light are the eight black crystal holograms. She smiles until her lips bleed. She plays the game perfectly. Miniature twin horses float in the air above her hands.

But it's not enough. She needs the sensation again. She needs more. Mom considers eating the black crystal, all of it.

Horizontal bars of orange and pink stack inside each horse's body and a river of creatures – snails, rabbits, birds, snakes – connect their mouths. *In this family the loss begins with you.* Above the horses the black crystal holograms form a dark field bordered by a pulsating heat. *I don't feel solid anymore.* When Mom leans forward the horses squeal and their legs come down and into the back of her neck. *Tell me there's more than reality.*

Mom, now sitting up, eyes crazy and filled with tears, lifts the box and smashes it on the floor between her legs. She raises it and brings it down again and again. She shakes her head from side to side and her hair tries to follow and blurs. She keeps smashing. Red arcs splinter the air. The horses disappear through portals. Gripping the black crystal like a pestle she grinds the box into the floor.

She slumps onto her side and lies gasping for air, covered in sweat, her gown transparent against her skin. She drops the black crystal. She moves her legs but her legs don't move. Hundred barks, his paws visible in the space between floor and door.

Her face sideways, one eye open and tear-filled, the other dark against the carpet, she grabs the crystal and pulls it toward her.

She opens her mouth and closes her eyes.

Her teeth come down on the crystal so hard her lower jaw shifts an inch to the left and her mouth balloons liquid. She eats. She's flooded with pictures. She looks inside her right lung and sees a garden inhabited by rabbits and a bear eating blueberries. Hidden in ragweed, a fox pops his head out and says she never was a very good mother, better to just leave and let Remy take her place. The bear walks with both hands outstretched, smearing blueberries on her ribs.

The carpet is rough as gravel and her face burns. She chews hard bits, not sure if it's black crystal or teeth. She sees herself running from the garden and across a beach and Tock Ocki is there, running with her, telling her she's one of the special ones, I told you, I told you that you'd be special, hey, slow down, look at that. For a moment, she sees numbers racing past a thousand as a road coming out of the ocean and connecting to the sun.

11

He is led down a blue hall by four guards. His body feels broken. When he steps down the flesh of his right ankle sinks into the heel of his foot, or at least it feels that way to Pants who is a total mess physically and soon-to-be mentally. With each step he takes he skips three. His right arm, in a sling, is signed by an inmate that says *your perception is your reality so just make it be whatever.* His head is wrapped in white bandages with a dark spot seeping through in the shape of a key. They stop at the end of the blue hall.

Jackson's Hole is four feet by four feet with a fourteen-foot-high ceiling containing four lines of light. The door becomes a concrete wall when it shuts. Pants sits on the floor with his head throbbing. He wonders what the record length for a headache is, how much of his skull had to be cleaned off the floor. He's not completely sure why he's here, but he has a basic understanding.

The administration's decision to place him in solitary is based on fear. Without black crystal they remove him from the population not to protect him from inmates, but from the guards who have become irritable and are acting strange. Yesterday a guard showed up to work in a gorilla costume spray painted in graffiti and another guard, seemingly drunk, held a dark-colored rock that he rabidly chewed while doing squat-thrusts. The guard with the gold cross has gone missing. His gold cross was found nailed to the mural of skeletons and roses. There has been talk of a riot not among inmates, but guards. They don't want to be themselves anymore, they want to get back outside themselves, to the version with the black crystal inside them.

Pants falls asleep on the concrete floor. It's probably due to the green medication they injected him with because his arm is covered in crystals and he tries to brush them away but they're ghosts. He's inside a white building. From a window he sees the prison and it's pretty with the lights on. The crystals on his arm are different sizes, and in certain spots, a large crystal has small crystals consisting of smaller crystals. He digs his arm. They snap off, turn to pulp between his rubbing fingers, change to the color of smoke, rise. Looking under his arm he picks at gold colored rock hanging blob-like from his skin. He curls his fingernails in, pulls and tears away thick layers of gold alive in dream.

A bed lines the length of his arm. On the bed are hundreds of identical horses filled with colored bars. When he shakes his arm they fall. The horses land on the prison floor and flail their legs in a struggle to stand. Thirteen different versions of Mom from childhood – thirteen images of her from his favorite moments including playing with her in the rain, and lying in bed while she read to him, and standing behind her while she cooked at the stove – jump from his arm and dive into the flooding fog from the horses' mouths. Then he runs across every floor in the white building, smashes out every window with a hammer, rides a coffin-sized and chain-powered elevator to new floors, to more windows that need smashing. He runs until he can't feel his legs. He runs until he's on the roof of the white building, the fog coming up and after him, horses squealing, guards fucking on white clouds in a million different positions above him saying to relax, it's all going to work out, we're all sky fathers here, grab a limb, join us.

It's dark when he wakes. He's torn the sling off his arm and also the head bandages. His arm, from inner wrist to armpit, is shredded like forked meat. Puss colored blue with weak sparkle drips from his elbow. If Z. comes back with black crystal he'll be able to see the family he loves, dislikes, needs, wants to connect with once more before his body turns to husk. He can't forgive himself. He can't get outside himself.

The sun wants to swallow the earth not for reasons of expansion, but attraction to the black crystals. The universe will not miss the earth. There are billions of planets. The black crystals reach for the sun in a moving spider web, coming up from the earth's center, ready to break through all dirt, rock, grass, and bone.

10

A man is working in one of the tunnels. He looks familiar, but not familiar in the sense that he's a mine worker. Skip Callahan asks where his work clothes are and Z. says he forgot them at home, that everything he owns is saturated with dirt and sweat from working and the weather. Skip shrugs, not recognizing Z. from the table in the street incident, but still thinks they've met before. He considers asking if he knows him from Eddies or if he's a member of Brothers Feast who Skip has always actively ignored. At first Skip decides on saying nothing. He's impressed at how hard Z. is working because the heat wave has slowed everyone. He watches and tells himself to back off, let this man work, don't upset him, but he can't help himself.

Skip says, "Might want to consider going shirtless. It's my move, but you can have it."

"Thanks," says Z. "I'm new here. Thank you."

"Doesn't matter," says Skip. There's a break in his thinking, his eyes kind of glazing over. Then: "Have we met?"

"Parents worked here. You know my father, Richard? We look the same. This is his idea. Mom says we have the same bone structure, something about our foreheads. We cross our legs the same way when we sit. Drives her nuts when we're watching the TV."

"At Eddies?"

"I don't drink. And I don't forget a face."

Skip studies the man before him and thinks maybe it's the heat, or the shock from seeing a girl run like a dog, an image that continuously haunts him, because his mind keeps breaking, keeps going black like he's passing out for a few seconds here and there and then coming back into a gauzed reality. He can't sleep at night. He stares at walls. He's impressed that someone is not only working, but working so hard in the heat wave. The call for more workers – parchment nailed to trees and public bathrooms – was put out weeks ago and too few new faces have arrived. The village dims in evening because workers are mining less yellow and the city has taken notice, men at newly installed binocular stations writing in lined notebooks noting it as a weakness, another reason it should be overtaken. There's a "binocular station attendant" dressed in blue who walks back and forth, nodding and smiling in a depressed kind of way.

Z. knows what to say, how to change Skip's eyes. "What matters is work," he says. "Dad always told me that if you're not working, then you're not working."

Skip goes, "Ha!"

Z. finds a pick-ax. The workers stay away because Z. is insane with motion and he's making them look bad. When the evening aims for dark, the workers gone for the day and shaking their heads in disbelief over pints of ale at Eddies at the man who accomplishes more than five of them combined, Z. uses the pick-ax to break into a shed. He steals a helmet with a light and a shovel with a short handle. Before running back into the tunnel he stops and looks up at the sky. From a great distance, looking down from where Z. stares, *is that a star, maybe that's a star*, he is tiny standing in the mine, almost unnoticeable, nearly nothing. He stops looking up when he suddenly enters a coughing fit. The air is a black oven. Bugs drip from the sky and Z. has swallowed one.

Inside the tunnel he stabs the dirt wall with the shovel where his hands and pick-ax previously clawed. He digs until he forms a door. He digs until he's working in a hallway. He throws piles of dirt behind him until he's so deep inside he has to walk piles out. Soon he's traveling through another hallway, this one too lacking black crystal. When he finds yellow, or blue, he tosses them into separate piles for the trucks to gather in the morning. He works until he can't lift his arms.

He sleeps huddled in a fetal position against a wall of dirt which is surprisingly cool and comforting.

He wakes, rolls onto his side with rocks piercing his skin, and vomits something red. His count is lowering with having to live. With slits for eyes caked closed with dirt he walks from the mine tunnel and into the low sunshine of morning to workers drinking coffee from ceramic mugs. They roll their eyes at Z., sneer dirt, then go back to their conversations about what will happen to them, what's the deal with the sun, what's your number. Even in morning the heat is shocking.

Skip Callahan walks past. "Saw a girl running like a dog once. Like, a real dog, on all fours and everything. Everyone, yeah you, gives me a hard time for talking about it. Keeps me up at night because I only wanted to help, see if she was okay. I think of going back to the house but what would I say? You're like a mole and we need more moles. Jesus, you worked all night, huh? Don't need another person who sits around drinking coffee," says Skip, the last few words louder and directed at the workers.

Z. smiles, looks worried.

"Thanks," says a worker to Z. "THANK YOU FOR HELPING!"

The workers climb into gun metal trucks and drive into the tunnels. Some grab shovels leaning against idling trucks and walk in. The clang and bang of machines, hammers. When Z. looks up from left to right the sky scans from red to white.

9

ad enters Remy's room and says Mom has one remaining. He tells her to leave her alone because something has happened to her mouth. Remy sits atop a mountain of pillows on her bed. She's drawn pictures of black crystals all over the walls and ceiling. Where the red crystal once was, with the baby inside, has been blackened in scramble.

"We should just go."

"Can't," says Dad.

"Why? Because of the fence? Because of Adam? Sorry. Actually, I'm not. I don't think there's anything in this world that can't be said. Just because we're different from them doesn't mean we're bad. It doesn't mean we can't try to save her. They are coming in anyways."

"It doesn't matter where we go because you can't reverse what is happening to her."

"You see everything as dying."

Remy moves forward on the mountain of pillows which are balanced in a way so she slides down and lands on her feet with a jump. Dad extends his hands like he's going to catch her but she stands tall, doesn't need his help. From outside, Remy hears something. She makes a *shhhhhhhh* sound with a finger over her lips and Dad turns toward the window. Running circles around the house is Hundred barking at the sun. He speeds past the window like black liquid, red sky behind him. He disappears for a few moments, the barking going small, the red sky appearing touchable, then reappears, a noisy smear going past the window.

"I'm sorry," says Dad.

"I'm sorry too."

"You are?"

"I'm sorry we never tried everything we could to save Mom."

Dad climbs to the roof and watches the city lights come on. They look brighter. The heat turns his shirt transparent with sweat and in several random places on his body he picks the fabric off his skin. The only thing he has to think about is her. He considers going to the hospital where people are rumored to be pumped full of crystals (Chapter 14, Resurrection, City Hospital Myth) but that means making a decision. Besides, he's never believed in the myth. It means taking a risk instead of just letting time decide. He understands what her face says without her saying a thing, that she wants to go. He's spent so much time doing nothing for her because everything stays inside him and rings his head and the grip of his thoughts can't get any tighter. And then there's Remy, what she wants him to do.

He sits with his knees drawn into his eye sockets and wishes he could move himself to tears because he feels crystals crushing, buildings burning, dogs dying. Inside, he is a blubbering mess, but outside he's a man who just can't show it. He was never like this in Younger Years. He spoke more. He expressed himself with chosen words and hand gestures. There was a time when Mom asked how he was feeling and without hesitation he gave an honest answer, not a reply like *good*. He once told her while sitting on the edge of the bed with his face in his hands that he felt depressed, don't laugh, something was wrong. He described his body as cement filled and horizontal. On some days he didn't speak to anyone until he got home and said hello, how was your day, the words leaving his body feeling alien. He said he was an awful father and husband because the way he was limited her and Remy, their life. Back then he spoke openly, and he remembers the way he was. That version would go to the city.

Beneath the roof Remy stands in Mom's room. On the bed her body and face are covered in a sheet. Where her mouth is, a black oval. Dad has placed a green crystal on her chest and a red on her stomach. With each breath the wet oval of her mouth expands then collapses. Remy stands motionless, watching the sheet move up and down. There's a silence. The room is surprisingly cool. Remy can't understand why Dad won't do anything, she's at the end, it's gone on too long, they can't keep watching this. She thinks about lifting her up right there and running to the city, saving her. She thinks about entering the hospital and being bathed in green light. But this is it, they will watch her become zero because of tradition. Remy runs away.

Under the blanket Mom's hands move up her body. It takes minutes to pull the sheet from her face, but Remy is already outside as dog-child – her and Hundred running into the mine where a man digging never-ending tunnels swears at walls of dirt. The air outside the sheet feels cool and new. Her mouth is broken. She tries to say something, the letters are bobbing inside her head like jellyfish, but she can't arrange them correctly.

8

He screams into the wall. He kicks the wall. Inmates think the noise is the heat wave howling against the prison and moving them closer to the village. There's a general uneasiness with Pants in isolation, a vibe amongst inmates that something holy is about to be destroyed. Their orange jumpers and blue shirts are damp and wrinkled. They listen to the howling and wait.

The guards take turns looking at the road for Z. to come back with his hands weighted to his thighs with black crystal. Jug imagines Z. carrying a crystal so massive he has to walk sideways through the door. A crystal so big Little Karl will fall off his chair, his book of | sent flying. More than half the guards don't show for work anymore, they are crazies running through the streets, painting their bodies with black crystals and black crosses. Those who do show up hate themselves for being themselves, but they keep it together, they gather their paychecks. They believe, in a religiously devoted sense, that Z. will come back to them, that Jug has done the right thing. The idea of Z. never returning is a cruel joke, and those who make it are ignored.

Pants asks passing footsteps if they're going to let him die in here and the silence means yes. His imagination is turning at an uncontrollable and sickening pace. What distracted him before was black crystal. He has to define his life some other way now. And with each thought comes layers of thoughts over that thought. How exhilarating to be a child. He never wondered then when his body would register zero and all color would leave his body, mouth, eyes. No need to acquire things. The days were an endless blur of games played in water and grass. The days, like what was inside, were never counted.

He mumble-sings *Gimme gimme crystal (pop pop) gimme gimme bark bark (woof woof)* and feels insane. He imagines baby Remy walking through the house. She fell down the stairs and broke her arm and he wonders what damage that must have done (-5). He remembers showing baby Remy the crystal mine, and how she sat in the black dirt molding clumps that soon rained from her spread fingers, and later, how she licked the glittering dust off her arms. He remembers killing a wounded bird because he wanted to experience, what he said to Mom, a little death, not too much, but enough to feel it. He wanted to try and move, with his shoe, the body of something once living.

He told Remy The Sky Father Gang would perform a demonstration like never before. She made a motion with her hands that symbolized city fireworks and he said no, not exactly, but just as thrilling, just you wait. They sat on his bed and when she saw the duffel bag packed with crystals she went *Ew yucky*. But he wasn't present in the moment, he didn't make eye contact. And there wasn't glowing light coming from the bag, spotlighting baby Remy's face. And there weren't loving words said by him because he would miss her. And there wasn't any true emotion conveyed at all because he had Dad inside him. When he kissed her on the head it felt choreographed, something he saw on television, which was true.

He vomits into his hands and looks for forty. His mind narrows in on the moment with Remy in his bedroom that at the time was so meaningless to him because he was young, and foolish, and he doesn't go sad with emotion, but it's anger with no place to go but from a pit in his chest and down to his stomach and through his legs and out his feet that kick the wall.

7

Z. climbs into a yellow machine that digs 10,000 times faster than the short-handled shovel. He creates so many tunnels he becomes lost. His head moves left to right and back again. He reverses the digging machine, climbs out, and inspects the walls with his hands. He's covered in dirt and sweat. He jumps back into the machine, begins working again, and every time he reverses the ceiling rains rocks. He drives and digs, drives and digs, his mind a wet hornet on the fact that he needs to find the black crystal to not only save the Brothers, but to accomplish something that every child has dreamed about since the beginning of time. All his energy is placed in forward movement.

The machine, which is old and rattles with loose parts, is equipped with a shield-shaped light on the top that blazes the path Z. digs. The light misses corners. Z. stops, leaps from the machine, and uses a flashlight to closely inspect shadows. He can't afford to be sloppy and miss what he needs. Beneath his feet he cracks yellow, blue, and green. He's surprised by a red. His body is a field of gravel. He crosses his arms and rubs his forearms together until a mound of gunk falls off.

He leans against the machine. He moves the flashlight over his body and up and down the tunnel walls. The air is hot, heavy, and where the flashlight misses it's dark with an occasional mist of gnats. Dust engulfs all space and the engine is at a low and rumbling growl. His concentration loosens, and for the first time since he began digging, he's forced to reflect on who he is, what he's doing, and his body deflates. He doesn't feel like a solid person anymore. His arms ache and his hair is matted with sweat. His fingernails are black with work. He's a person.

He aims the flashlight in the opposite direction of the machine. The light ends ghost-like where the tunnel splits into three different directions. He presses his head into the tunnel wall until rocks pierce his skin. He turns his back to the wall and sits on the ground where the air is so full of shit that when he opens his mouth to drink from a canteen his tongue is blanketed. He pulls his legs in and cleans his eyes with his knees. He tries to calm his shaking legs by massage. *What horrible things are happening to them?* With his tongue he cleans his front teeth. He swallows dirt and grips his calves. He's digging a tunnel to nowhere and in the thought, the clichéd metaphor for life of *digging a tunnel nowhere*, he laughs.

What does it all mean, and the thoughts go more sentimental: *wonder when I'll die, a body as husk, a body as zero. Will anyone remember me? HAHAHAHA.*

He once prided himself as someone who didn't think these thoughts. He mocked people who expressed feelings. But here, in this dark tunnel exposed by flashlight and machine light (*what happens when these lights burn out?*) his thoughts are inescapable. *You have to keep moving because it's the only thing a person can do.* He pulls himself up and into the machine and extends the tunnel.

Dig.

Breaks a new layer of wall.

Dig.

There's no black crystal.

Dig.

A waterfall of dirt attacks him.

Dig.

Z. ducking even though he's covered by the metal roof of the machine.

It doesn't exist so just get a dark-colored red, a bunch, and trick them.

When Z. was a child he met Adam McDonovan who told him he was breaching the city to achieve something no one had ever done before. Z. asked if it would be bigger than fireworks and he said yes, different, why was everyone talking about fireworks. He said that the true way to extend one's count was to have others remember you. He held a bag with dark crystals, looked like red. Everyone wants to be amazing in an ordinary world, said Adam. Z. listened and memorized every word. He didn't want to be stomped out like some bird. Just be great enough so someone younger will remember you, said Adam.

6

The division began with the night of separate bedsheets. For years, Younger Dad insisted on sleeping under the same sheets *because that is what married couples do*, no matter how much sheet Younger Dad took in twists during the night. Sometimes, Younger Mom woke with her fingers touching an edge of blanket as Younger Dad, deep in dream, held the blanket from her.

"Why's it such a big deal," said Younger Mom. "How do you expect me to sleep if I don't have any covers and you have to, absolutely *must*, sleep with a window open?"

Younger Dad had a theory that he'd achieve a better sleep if fresh air was blowing in. He spent his days working in the crystal mine, harvesting yellow and melting it down. It was difficult, messy work, that clogged his body. If fresh air wasn't circulating, his mouth and nose went dry and would cause him to wake throughout the night. Not that he could remember, the next day, of waking up, but he said he *felt it*. He said the sleep *didn't catch right*.

"What about a bigger blanket?"

"That's not a solution."

He took three blankets into the garage and placed them on the table where Harvak would one day expel his last crystal, and using a needle and black thread, he stitched. It took two

28

hours and the stitching was poor. When Younger Dad pulled at the new seams triangle-shaped holes formed. He went back and added thread – quick loops to help hold together the triple blanket that wasn't a solution, but an attempt.

He pulled the blanket from the garage and into the house where he let it drag across the floor and up the stairs. The blanket extended from the bottom of the stairs to the top and into the bedroom where it slithered from a fearful Remy who watched half-hidden, but standing, in her bedroom.

It took another hour to figure out how to display the blanket. The trick was to fold it in a way so it appeared to be three separate blankets stacked. He wanted it to be a surprise when Younger Mom entered the room, ready for bed, dressed in her gray nightgown, brushing her teeth with one hand while pulling the bedsheet down with the other.

"What's going on here?" she asked, looking at the bed stacked high with blankets.

"Watch THIS," Younger Dad said.

He pulled one layer off and to the right and another to the left. The blanket touched each wall of the bedroom. One side had to be folded back over. Younger Dad stood with his arms extended outward.

"Very you," said Younger Mom smiling with her hand spread over her mouth. "Still going to keep the window open?"

That night, on each respected side, they crawled into bed and under the blanket with a good fifteen feet of fabric on each side.

Yes, the window was open. Yes, Younger Mom was smiling and laughing. Yes, Younger Dad felt pure joy for having injected pure joy into Younger Mom. Yes, Younger Dad asked if Younger Mom was tired and ready for sleep and she said yes and yes they went to sleep. They were years away from the first signs of her illness but it was there, inside her. It didn't matter then. There was joy in that bed.

Younger Mom woke at 2:35 in the morning because of the

breeze blowing on her arms. The blanket had dipped to her waist. She pulled it to her chin, fell back asleep, only to wake twenty minutes later with the edge of the blanket against the side of her body.

"It worked," Younger Dad said in the morning, a spoon filled with oatmeal raised to his lips. "I'm good."

"Not exactly," she said, pouring a cup of coffee, looking through the kitchen window above the sink. "Put all the blanket on my side tonight."

So, they put all the blanket on Younger Mom's side in a ridiculously huge pile even Harvak was too scared to jump into. Younger Dad had barely enough blanket to cover his body. He had about two inches of blanket on his side, to the thirty feet of clump on Younger Mom's.

It didn't work.

"I'm sorry," said Younger Dad. "Huh."

They tried tucking the blanket under the mattress, and they tried wrapping Younger Mom in a tunnel of blanket, and they even tried having Younger Dad only touching the edge of the blanket, not even on him really, but none of it worked. The last attempt involved Harvak sleeping between them – the dog acting as a kind of anchor to the blanket. But after an hour Younger Dad flipped and flopped and Harvak leaped from the bed as the blanket shifted once again and the breeze blew in from the open window.

"People talk about people who don't sleep together," he said.

"You should care about me sleeping, not people."

"I believe in a one blanket policy, I think," said Younger Dad.

That night Younger Dad went into the bedroom and saw two blankets – one brown and one white – neatly folded side by side on the bed.

Years passed. Remy grew. Adam imprisoned. Mom coughed a new sound. Dad fought through his blanket. That is, instead of taking blanket, which he couldn't do now, his body moved toward the center of the bed and pushed at Mom who woke throughout the night from knees and elbows.

"Last night your elbow pressed into my spine."

Dad tried sleeping on the couch. He couldn't fall asleep because the flow of air from the window wasn't right. Mom tried too, but the couch proved too lumpy, and she hated the feeling of her arm disappearing between cushions.

"It's temporary," she said. "What we'll do is set up a bed in the spare bedroom. I know, his bedroom. I'll get some sleep. My head hurts."

"If that's what you want," said Younger Dad. "If sleeping in separate bedrooms is a good idea then let's do it."

Dad stands on the roof. He kept the triple blanket in the garage for years, and earlier, pulled it up the ladder. It hung blob-like over the eaves and became a flag some villagers waved at when Dad shook-out the dust. He placed it over the roof, corners to corners. Wondering what to do about Mom – can anything living be saved from death – the triple blanket covers all.

5

emy runs through the mine with Hundred. Sharp yellow disregarded by workers because they won't liquefy due to over-crystallization cut her feet. Remy imagines her count as twenty ice cubes pyramided inside her. *I don't have any color. Mom is leaving. Who will be strong enough to bury her body? Dad is with her now, he will watch her go.* Leaving the mine, Remy looks toward the city so near, the fence smashed by three new buildings. The sun is a predator in its sky blistering. She heads home feeling helpless.

Dad climbs down from the roof by way of ladder holding the triple blanket.

"You're not with her?"

Dad bunches the blanket against his face, trying to keep it from hitting the dirt, but most of it remains clumped at his feet. "Going in now."

"To see if she's dead?"

"To check."

"Just help her. Let's go. Come on, please."

Dad walking toward the front door: "I'm doing everything I can."

"You're not doing anything."

"Remy."

"You'll be remembered for doing nothing."

"Who will remember?"

"Me."

"Stop it."

"I'll stop when you help her. This has been going on for too long. Please."

"Remy, I told you."

"Let me see her face."

"No."

"I'm going to see her face before she's gone, you owe me that."

"You shouldn't see her like this."

"You can't stop me."

She follows Dad into the house where he dumps the triple blanket on the couch. They walk to Mom's room, Remy stepping on the heels of Dad. The house is heavy with heat and difficult to navigate. Things are melting: a diamond-print reclining chair holds the impression of a giant, and the flesh-toned paint on the walls is dripping on the floor. When they enter the bedroom their bodies move slower in her presence. Mom looks tiny on the bed. Dad removes the blanket from her face in a quick passive-aggressive sort of way, looking at Remy the entire time, as if he knows what her reaction will be, as if he knows, and doesn't care, that it will hurt her.

"You wanted to see."

Remy's shoulders fold inward and her stomach absorbs a hammer. Sharp pieces of crystal trickle down inside her. She's never seen a body get this far.

Mom's face has lost meat the skull once held. And Dad was right, something is wrong with her mouth, as if she chewed bricks. Her eyes are glazed and rust-colored. Soon, her left eye will drip crystals (Chapter 5, Death Movement, Book 8). Her nose is hardened ash that Remy imagines if she touched would crumble. Gray hair gunked with shit fans her pillow. Dad repeats *Can you hear us? Can you? Are you okay?* and Remy thinks *Don't leave me*. Smell of dead dogs. Smell of burning. She peels the blanket from Mom's feet and sees the skin is a darker red compared to her face and neck, and even her veins, once strong and blue, have disappeared beneath this new red shell. *A lack of circulation results in the color red drying everything up, erasing the last crystals in the body* (Chapter 9, Death Movement, Book 8). The red is moving toward her chest and aiming to stop her heart.

"You don't have to be here," says Dad, in a softer tone now that he's seen Remy's reaction. "I know you've heard this before, from me, from books, and maybe you don't believe it, but it's never been disproved. Parents go and their children step into their place. There's nothing wrong with just letting that happen."

The blanket on the bed, also significant in size but not quite triple blanket size, falls off the bed and to the floor. Shards of broken black crystal and blood dot the carpet and there's something resembling half a tooth. Remy wants to pick up the black pieces and eat them. Mom's face is turned up to the ceiling, throat exposed and seemingly not moving with breath.

"Do something," says Remy.

"But I can't," Dad says.

"Let's just go."

"No."

"Come on. Like you said, it doesn't matter."

Dad kisses Mom on the forehead and her throat moves. He turns his ear toward her mouth and listens. Remy can't hear her, but whatever the words are, whatever the sound does, it makes Dad put his hand over his mouth and nose like he can block the emotion from coming out. He speaks into her ear. A block of melted ceiling crashes on the floor next to the bed but Dad doesn't notice because he puts his ear back on her mouth and listens. He cries and then laughs, nodding. He rubs her head then says more, none of it audible for Remy to pick up on other than her name and Adam and the word *younger*. When Dad listens again it's just sick person air. Maybe she's smiling, with her lips like that. Dad turns to Remy, his body still leaning over Mom and says, "She's such a – " He turns back to Mom. "Okay," he says. "We'll go."

"Yes!"

Remy immediately feels embarrassed for being so excited.

"We'll figure out how to navigate the city. We have nothing to lose, you're right. I don't care if we get arrested. Okay, let's go."

"It's going to work," says Remy. "I can feel it."

Dad picks Mom up and feels the odd non-weight of her body. Seemingly unhinged, her head flops back.

"Careful," says Remy, and moves in to support her head.

Before they leave Dad puts Mom back down on the bed and covers his face with two hands. He can't handle it anymore. The emotion is pushing him around. But Remy is ready. She's been waiting for this. She picks Mom up in the blanket and says it's going to be okay, they won't let her die, the city has powers (Chapter 14, Resurrection, City Hospital Myth). Thumb and finger around the bridge of his nose, eyes closed, Dad makes a snarl-face, inhales, and composes himself, says okay, just be careful with her. The house is full of hot disease and it throbs – walls, ceilings, floors – beating inward. Another block of melted ceiling, it appears saturated with water, crashes near the closet. Remy holds Mom to her body in the blanket. She's so light. Remy unfolds wrinkles of fabric to find her legs which are tucked up to her chest and look like dried fruit.

She has at least one left.

"Ready?"

"Yeah."

Remy exits the bedroom with Dad following like Remy followed him before into the house, Dad now the one stepping on Remy's heels.

Outside, and walking quickly with the city in the near distance, everything is blowing dirt and bugs and heat. Most people are hiding inside, but a few dozen are out in the streets, watching.

An elderly woman wears necklaces of green crystals that cover her entire neck, bracelets of blue and yellow from wrist to elbow on both arms. She stands on a rock and screams at the buildings. She smirks at Remy and Dad and Hundred. She tells them that everything comes for the village because the village is pure, this is the end of times, soon nothing will exist but dirt and it's going to be better. Remy tells her to get inside, protect your number, you crazy.

The temperature today will shatter records with the sky creamed. They just need to keep moving toward the hospital and they won't notice their dehydration, their exhaustion. A group of villagers point at three buildings built directly on top of the fence and there seems to be dozens of skyscrapers in the near distance too. Remy holds Mom closer. Dad walks beside them. They move toward the fence.

Mom's weight increases when she suddenly stretches her legs out. The blanket trips Remy who stumbles but keeps her balance. More dirt and dust blows through the air and she squints, makes sure the blanket covers Mom. Dad offers to carry her. Remy says no, she does this, and Dad says okay, just please, be careful. They check her breathing by gazing into her mangled mouth, listening for wheeze and air. If this smell, like dead dogs, an odd sourness burning, is part of the death process, Remy's never read about it, only experienced it from Harvak and smelled it on Mom that day in the kitchen. Her left eye drips a skinny trail of red.

"She's close," says Remy.

They run.

The sky isn't a sky because the sky is a sun.

They run.

The sky isn't like skin.

They run.

The sky is shit.

They run.

Dad loses his balance before standing still with his arms

braced outward and he says *Hold on, the ground tilted. Is this really the end of everything?* He's sure of it, the ground moved.

Remy stops. The towering buildings are scattershot in her vision because of the heat and swirling dirt. Windows are black boxes containing the faint outlines of nine-to-five workers eating ham sandwiches and discussing what they'll have for dinner. She felt something move too, her feet trembled, but isn't sure what, and figures it's her own exhaustion, lowering count, causing her to lose her balance like Dad. She waits to feel something move beneath her but there's nothing.

"We can't keep stopping," she says. "Come on."

Remy pulls the blanket over Mom's head before running again. She's incredibly fast, much practice in the mine. Dad runs several steps behind, to the side. He concentrates on the tails of blanket sweeping Remy's feet and Hundred darting around them, biting them. Can't have Remy trip and drop Mom so he yells at Hundred, feels like he's doing something important when really the dog has never listened to him. The ground tilts again. Dad slows down, a sad little trot because he doesn't want to stop but he's tired and has that side/back pain he's had since the truck accident. Besides, the ground is trembling, he's sure of it.

"Hurry," Remy says, nearing the fence.

"The ground."

"I know, just, come on."

Those in the village shield their eyes from the sun. Growing smaller in the distance – Remy, Dad, and Hundred. Standing at the fence is Skip Callahan, crouched and holding up a section of peeled open fence, a pair of wire cutters next to his boot, his hands covered in thermal burns, a giant grin plastered over his face telling them to hurry up, he's always wanted to help, come on.

4

He sits with his knees drawn to his chest, arms wrapped around his legs. He's playing Mom memories. She let them play in the mud during a rainstorm. Pants laughed in his soaked clothes and Mom said she'd clean them up later. The sky was a feathery gray. Dad isn't in the memory because Dad was somewhere else. Mom bounced baby Remy in her arms as baby Remy covered her eyes with forked fingers, partially protected from the rain, but wanting to see the outside world, the movement of raindrops, light. He can still smell the mud.

But he can't avoid the later Mom memories. Dinner table fights. Slammed doors. All those angry clichés proving true and hurting. The evening when she went after him with flailing fists and he had to restrain her against a wall, and how that moment triggered the night he saw her with the robed men. He pressed her fists into the wall, the wall *thudded*, and Dad asked from his bedroom *Is everything okay in there?* but didn't get up. He was in bed eating eggs. Mom said to stop and twisted her head from side to side and he couldn't stop because he was so scared from what he had to do. He pushed her onto the bed and ran.

Then he plays the night he can't process. The night he discussed during the health meeting. He sees her with the men in dark robes who at the time, at his young age, possessed a creature-like quality with pawing claws and freakish hip sways. Or maybe that was his imagination because in his revisiting of the memory he isn't watching from a distance, he's standing there as one of them. He puts his hand inside his mouth and screams. His eyes hurt from his voice. There is no key to life only doors. He rolls on the floor and watches Mom with the men so close he could comb her hair. When it's his turn, when the men with their evil green grins tell him *Get it, son, don't stop, get it get it,* Pants crawls to the corner of the cell and balls himself up until he can push his neck into the wall by extending his legs against the other wall. He wants to get back inside the memory of the rainstorm, of being a boy again, but each time he tries to focus on his reflection in the puddles, Mom's gown soaked at the very bottom, his bare feet running through wet grass, the calmness he felt knowing nothing about death, it's all shredded by the hands of the men. In this version they're from the city, just dressed like villagers, just trying to make things worse for the village, just trying to make it feel unsafe so the city is a hero riding in, and Pants thinks yes, that's who it was all along.

He can't turn his head off. When his neck can't be pressed further, his legs fully extended, his body goes limp and he rolls onto his back. For a moment, he sees nothing, and that feels good. Hands on his chest he breaths in bursts that raise and lower his chest in such a dramatic fashion that he screams for help even though he knows the guards can't hear him or don't care to. He thinks he should have been a better son, and should have been a better brother, but he did the best he could, and it's only in this present moment, looking back, can he think such a non-helpful thought as *I should have done better.* In the past you can change yourself into someone better, or worse, but not in the present moment, no, that's impossible because the memory can't be molded yet into what you want it to be, and Pants thinks this,

17

and laughs, and he moves his hand across the always cool prison floor imagining the dirt from the crystal mine as he breaks apart a layer of static.

3

After he hits something hard, the machine abruptly stopping, the back two wheels bouncing up a few inches and jarring Z., he jumps out. A cloud of dust and debris takes a moment to clear. He looks under the machine for broken machine parts. He's a mud mask with white eyes. He swallows another bug, a lightweight thing consisting of only wings, and waits for visibility to return inside the tunnel he's created. He stares at the wall.

In front of the machine he crouches at the wall and uses the flashlight to form a head-sized white circle around a protruding spike. Tilting the flashlight up, down, left to right, the spike gleams. One side appears mirrored, and Z. doesn't even recognize himself. He licks his lips and tastes dirt. A triangular section of the spike is smooth as glass. Using his fingers, he digs a little deeper into the wall, around the base of the spike, and dirt pours around what becomes a crystal. The more dirt that falls away the wider it becomes. He can't believe what he's seeing. He wonders what it tastes like, what it can do to a person, how is this possible.

He grabs tools from the machine. He moves faster now, trembling with excitement. Here he is, someone who has discovered something thought never to have existed. He picks and digs. The crystal is double the size of his torso and it's an unmistakable solid black. The light from the machine flickers, makes a terrible short-circuiting sound, and Z. turns to the change in light like it's a bottle breaking. He checks the flashlight propped up on a rock that he has aimed in his direction. It's already going to be impossible to find his way out of here, he can't have the lights go. He imagines driving aimlessly through the tunnels, a flashlight held in his mouth, the machine full of black crystal rumbling through darkness, dirt swells, bug colonies.

He raises the hammer.

He breaks off fist-sized chunks. Clanging echoes reverberate through his arms. There's gunk in his nose and he blows it out on his right arm, then raises the arm, aims, comes down and breaks off another chunk. He only needs so much to bring back but the more he gets, the bigger the hero he is or something, or so he thinks in the moment, so he cracks off more ham-sized pieces and leaves the remaining black crystal protruding from the wall. He can't stop smiling. He wonders how far the crystal extends, maybe a network of black roots covering miles.

He places the chunks in the back of the machine where the toolbox is. Then the light on the machine burns out in a burst. Everything goes dark. Z. makes a noise he's never heard before.

He sits in the idling machine with a narrow path of light filled with dust extending from his mouth where he holds the flashlight. *How deep am I?* He hears footsteps. *Why has no one come?* He jumps from the machine again and walks to where the remaining black crystal is and puts his ear against the wall, one hand flat against a cool side of the crystal. Through the wall gritty and cutting against his ear there's water rushing through sewers, cars accelerating under yellow lights.

2

They run in a nightmare of heat and dust. Everything looks red. The sun pierced by buildings wrapped in tornadic filth. Flames as kites are being pulled endlessly from the windows of several burning buildings and men below in red and gold helmets aim their hoses skyward where the water's arc disappears just as it begins. Newspapers, umbrellas, plastic bags, fast food cartons, black flies, clumps of hair, dirty diapers, spaghetti, magazines, a million types of colored garbage, all blow across the sky. There's a howling. It's so loud because in the city everything makes a noise. Their eyes sting with sweat. They squint as they run.

Into the city streets scattered with people they run. Cabs, motorcycles, sidewalk corners crowded with men who stand in the sweltering heat wearing suits – their faces expressionless shining with sweat in the sun. There is a store that sells just coffee. There is a store that sells just cheese. There is a store that sells just pie. A man holding a plastic plate holding a slice of pie takes a bite and his eyes widen. He turns to his wife and says, "Fresh apples," while pointing to the pie with his fork. She tries the pie and nods while chewing. After she swallows she says, "Really fresh."

Remy overhears someone say that the city is moving, it's crawling over the village now because it's destiny, it's what god wants, hooray! The man stops people by placing his hands on their shoulders. He asks if they've seen his gold cross necklace. Everyone shrugs him off and the man keeps running, starts tackling people. City people hate touching so the man is their worst enemy. Eventually three cops stop him, the man saying he's a cop too, hey, stop that, until he goes quiet in the mush.

City people wear fancy t-shirts. City people don't show their fear. Babies are pushed in carts by parents in sunglasses so you can't guess their count. City people run for fun and call it jogging. The howling sound dips lower and pummels legs with wind. Again, the ground moves.

"Hurry," Remy says, and they cross a street, dodging cars and bicycles.

City people scream with blood-red faces and slap the air with their fists. "You wait for the man to glow in the box to tell you when to walk," says a small angry woman to Remy and Dad as they cross, the woman's facial expression stoic in the blowing filth. "That's what you do."

"You tell 'em, Mom," says a man standing next to her.

A car tire comes an inch from running over Remy's heel and she leaps onto the sidewalk, tilting Mom a little, but not dropping her. Dad says to be careful and puts his hand on her back, pulling her further from the street, but not really doing anything, Remy already jumped. They have no idea where they are going but the hospital is somewhere and there's an end point they are working toward. The small angry woman begins crossing the street while walking bent forward at a severe angle, the wind pushing her back, her will stronger and pushing her forward, facial expression not changing even as she peels, with finger and thumb, a plastic bag with a red smiling face with pigtails, from her own face, her other hand holding the grown man's hand and seemingly pulling him along to an undesirable appointment.

Remy bounces Mom in her arms as she runs. Hundred barks at the end of a street lined with trucks that sell food to long lines of impatient people. A man with a chrome cart sells a product called hot dogs that float in bins of hot water, little puffs of steam rising each time the lid is taken off. The chrome cart has a glossy red hot dog with legs and the hot dog is smiling as a salivating mouth from the right chomps away at the hot dog's bun-clad body. Remy thinks *They put that in their mouths.*

Another rumbling is felt through the soles of their feet, this one larger, this one knocking people to the ground who curse the sky while trying to stand back up. They look to see what new buildings are rising. They scream and laugh and cry. Everyone in the city is insane. Everyone is touching technology. Free space in the city doesn't exist. Every inch is filled, and from a cloud's view, it's all moving like a tidal wave of concrete and blinking lights toward the village.

"Moms should never be allowed to die because Moms are forever," says Remy, seemingly to no one, only concentrating on finding the hospital, her eyes trying to read the letters painted on windows. There's a store that sells just dog food.

"What?" says Dad.

"Moms are a void never to be filled."

"What are you saying? Slow down."

"We can't."

"Are we close?"

"Just come on."

The hospital is a towering white building of glass windows with a glowing +. It's so white it blinds through the red sky, the blowing filth of the city. Hoards of people stand outside the entrance. It's hurricane windy but many don't care. A woman in a wheelchair smokes a cigarette with her hair flying around her head like a baby's handwriting. She stares blankly ahead until she sneezes blood and smoke and loses her cigarette. A man dressed in green lights another and places it between her lips.

The earth shakes and blurs and Remy fights back tears as she runs holding her dying mom.

11

A half-naked man with his face covered in black crosses stands on a wooden box and yells, "THE SUN IS COMING TO CLEANSE US ALL, HALLELUJAH, THE SUN IS COMING TO CLEANSE US ALL," and the man selling hot dogs slaps the air. The half-naked man grins and drawn on each tooth is a black cross and the hot dog vendor looks scared. He continues to yell, "THE SUN IS COMING TO CLEANSE US ALL, HALLELUJAH, THE SUN IS COMING TO CLEANSE US ALL."

They run down street after street and Remy bleeds as people take pictures and upload videos.

Another ground trembling, another slight tilting of the universe, another inch the sun pushes in.

A collective moan as the sky vines with cracks.

"The sun is to blame," says a woman named Sharon or Carol or Tammy or Julie or Amy or Mom or Cathy or Kelly. "But you know something, I don't really know."

"Everyone is a falling number," says Remy. "Get inside, protect yourself."

A boy named Joey, the son of Sanders who has recently begun airing political ads claiming victory over the village says, "What's that?" and points.

In the center of an intersection a fountain of dirt sprays the sky with a rush like a stream grown after a storm. Men and women scatter away and clog up doorways. A man drops his phone, starts to go back for it, but is pulled away by his wife. Roads split and the earth tilts and those still standing don't wait to fall. From inside the fountain a giant yellow insect crawls upward.

"COME ON!" says Remy. "PLEASE COME ON!"

They sprint down a final area of sidewalk and reach the hospital, the fountain in the intersection still in partial view from the hospital entrance. *Mom is going to be saved.* There's a hotel attached to the hospital and there's a church attached to the hotel and all three are in a race to consume the most sky. Two men dressed in green standing at the sliding glass doors take the blanket and pull the fabric down to reveal her face. *Mom will be Mom forever.* They call, without emotion, for a stretcher. The woman in the wheelchair smoking, hair in the wind a fighting nest of odd angles, laughs at the sky and then coughs in a way that makes Remy think she's near zero. The two men look at Remy, ask if she's okay, and she nods. She hasn't seen what her feet look like. *Mom is safe now, don't worry about me.* One of the men looks Dad up and down, Dad trying to catch his breath, he's so out of shape, his stomach hurts, his back throbbing. But he also feels a strange kind of opening, something like success because they've made it.

"She's red because she's losing her final crystal," says Remy.

One of the men turns and looks at her. "What?"

"She's a red giant."

"What she's trying to say," says Dad, "is that she needs an injection, or whatever, to increase her count."

"Okay," says the other man, looking so totally lost that he smiles. "Wait, what?"

The stretcher arrives. They place Mom on it and enter the hospital. Dad stays outside because he can't stop looking at what's happening back in the intersection, the fountain growing taller, getting louder, more people screaming. He's completely distracted by something he's never seen before, that no one has seen before, all that dirt blowing into the air with this thing, this yellow insect, coming up and out of it.

"Wha," says Dad. "HOLY."

There's another eruption and triangular shapes of street bloom outward from inside the fountain of dirt and the yellow insect rises. It makes a high-pitched whining sound as it struggles to pull itself from the hole. Those on the ground crawl on their stomachs toward building entranceways where people scream to hurry, their heads filled with sci-fi endings. The wind shatters a bank's ATM window. A man crouches, holds his head, looks for his ATM card with the password LIZ&MONTY. The sun bends pavement. Laughing teens run in place, the wind holding them in place as they sink into the road. The yellow insect drags itself from the hole and becomes a machine with clumps of dirt spilling around it.

"How is that," says Dad.

Two black crystals fall off the back as the yellow machine rights itself with two final flops. The engine buckles with the changing of gears, the whine relaxes to a growl, and a part, looks like a rusty pipe, falls under a tire as the machine moves forward.

Z. is hunched over the wheel, covered in gunk, dirt still raining down all around him. A few rocks clang off the metal roof. He screams for everyone to get out of his way and swats the air wildly in front of him. The tires leave two trails of dirt clumps shaped like hexagons in the street as he drives, trying to remember where the prison is. Dad steps back, turns, and runs into the hospital.

Inside, orderlies and patients and doctors and janitors pressed to the walls allow a clear path for Dad to follow. Ahead of him is Remy. The walls are an endless smear of green. Dad has the weird expression of a man terrified but smiling, catching up to her and the wildly swerving stretcher disappearing around corners, then reappearing again and scaring old men glued to the walls, clutching their metal poles on wheels. He runs and feels himself come alive.

Doors fly open and inside are doctors with rubber-gloved hands. They turn their heads, their bodies not reacting. Freestanding fans blow hot air.

Then they take Mom in a sudden group effort. A hand grabs Remy's wrist and she slaps it away, runs to the table where they lay Mom, but Remy is pulled back again, this time by hands all over her body.

"Easy," says Dad.

The doctors in green move in smaller and faster packs around the room. They not only unwrap the blanket, but also put Remy on a table, who fights them off with flailing fists and feet – the feet what they are trying to inspect.

"Hey," says Dad. "Be careful with her. Don't touch her if she doesn't want you to."

Mom on the table is all bone. Her mouth is open under the white lights, her body motionless with electrical cords being attached to her red skin. There's so many white sheets. There's so many gray cords and clear bags with clear liquid hanging from metal rods like the old men in the hall had.

The doctors in green speak a different language.

A red light beeps in drip-like rhythm.

A black machine hooked up to Mom warms up with glowing green numbers – 76, 55, 40, 32, 80, 100, 74, 38.

Dad asks if those are what her count will be.

The doctors in green ignore him and inspect Remy's bloodied feet with tweezers. Again Dad speaks up, doesn't shut down, tells them to stop hurting her. Remy attacks them. *She's so strong.* Remy goes limp and slides off the table and runs to the door leaving behind bloody footprints.

"Give her one hundred," says Dad. "Please give her one hundred."

1

Driving in a straight line at a steady rate of speed, oblivious to his surroundings, machine maxed out and containing black crystals, Z. leaves the intersection of screaming people, burning buildings, blowing garbage, and heads to the prison. He finds the path the Brothers previously walked and the prison comes into focus through the swirling dirt in the final sky.

The guards see him coming from the prison windows. They've waited for this. They run down and open the gate. Little Karl drops his book.

He stops the machine and the guards circle around and begin inspecting the crystals. The only shine to Z. is a few clean teeth in his smiling head. One guard takes a razor, peels a layer of crystal off, and places it on his tongue. He smiles, says it's the right stuff, and Z. says as long as it's the right stuff he'll take them home.

Jug knocks on a crystal to hear if it's hollow, fake. He says this must be what remains and the ground trembles. He pats the largest piece and gives Z. a thumbs up.

The Brothers exit the prison shielding their eyes. Some limp and many have bruises ringing their necks. They straighten their curved backs and stand upright in the sunlight and then they do something Z. has never experienced before: applaud. The guards, his Brothers, and the village inmates walking from the prison all clap, whistle, and shout, and Z. bows and puts a hand in the air like *Okay, thank you, thank you very much, you don't have to do this you can stop now*, but he's so overwhelmed with emotion, he's been through so much, that his eyes fill with tears as he listens to the applause. He lets it wash over him. He notices how young the guards are. There's admiration in their eyes, and they keep shouting his name, and one guy makes an odd hooting noise while jumping and pumping a fist, and some guards slap Z.'s back and two guards, one for each leg, try to lift him up but they're too weak. Jug says he will be remembered forever now and the applause grows louder, seems to shake the ground. Jug will get his applause later. Z. takes another bow and smiles, this time blushing, not crying, this time thinking *I did it, yes.* He tries to guess the ages of the youngest guards.

Tall, scrawny, blond ponytail with top shaved head, Pants McDonovan exits the prison last. He claps and squints in the sun he hasn't felt in years. He licks his lips and tastes dirt and to him it tastes good, real. His skin looks dented. Black pools under both eyes, no sleep. When he sees a piece of black crystal he thinks about chomping down on a big edge right there but his lungs burn as they adjust to the air and he stands with both hands on his chest.

The guards carry the crystals inside. They walk hunched over in wide stances slobbering and pushing their crotches against it. There's enough for a lifetime and it's what they'll do, forever. They'll add inmates to keep the game going. Jug thinks about the party they will throw for him with no limits on coffee or donuts.

"Saw your Dad," says Z. "I was driving so fast and there was so much dirt and I'm so tired, but I think it was him walking into the hospital. We did it."

"How is everything not on fire," says Pants. "Are you sure?"

"He was standing outside the hospital next to a woman in a wheelchair."

"My head hurts."

"We're going to be remembered."

"But I don't feel alive."

"I never thought in a million years the black crystal existed. You should feel more than alive."

"What's a hospital? Was he okay?"

"It's a place people go to get injected with crystals," interrupts Bobby T., who stands but keeps losing his balance, his legs bruised from being hacked with batons, the ground again shaking. "I read that in Death Movement. He's in trouble."

"Listen," says Arnold, interrupting. "A hospital is suppose to help people. And Bobby T. is right, you should hurry."

"Where is it?"

0

Remy kicks a doctor in the throat. She's *been* kicking doctors in the throat. The doctor falls backward and slips in her blood. She spins and ducks from the grip of the others. She reaches for the door again.

Here he comes, dazed, light-headed, worried-eyebrows, never seen a place like this before, Brother.

"Who is this?" says one of the doctors. "Is he friend or family? SECURITY!"

"Adam," says Remy.

His orange jumpsuit is covered in black holes of sweat. He walks with a limp. His hair is matted with crusted blood from landing on a concrete floor. Transparent skin. His overall look is what you'd imagine someone to look like who spent days in solitary confinement, little light. Remy wraps her arms around his thighs and they both want to believe that their counts rise. They both want to slip backward in time, and together, here holding each other in the hospital with everything around them fogging away in green dream, they feel like children again. Adam pats Remy's head and kisses her. She imagines each pat adding one inside her. She feels so good in the swirling moment that the outside world is obliterated, it's just them now, they are together and bright now.

Adam looks at Dad and smiles, then sees Mom on the table

and realizes nothing is wrong with Dad at all, it's Mom, that's why they are here. It's been Mom this entire time. He's known this. He walks to the side of the table where she is, where a few doctors continue to work. One doctor stands against the wall. He's on the phone with the police. Each step is floating, as if walking through connected tunnels of dream. Adam touches her face with the backside of his hand and combs her hair to the one side it wants to go. He leans over, almost falls onto the table, and the doctors give space.

He slides his arms under and around her body, the hospital sheets cool against his skin, dirt cracking off his forearms. He lifts her from the table until his body and her body touch with her head resting on his shoulder. She weighs nothing. She is nothing. Against his ear her breathing sounds like mouth-blown mud. She smells sour with something inside burning and leaving. All her life, all her numbers, have led up to this point, this hospital reckoning. She's trying to remember all the good moments. She's trying to make sense of it all.

Remy walks over and supports Mom's head with her hands.

"It's okay," Adam says to Mom.

Her breathing gets louder.

"I'm here," he says.

He's a good one. He's a good one he's a good one I knew he'd be a good one he's a good one.

Her body jolts forward.

"No," says Adam. "I have you."

There's a Mom breath so deep that her chest expands into his chest. He feels the connection, the beating, the whatever it is inside them that makes them what they are. Two of the doctors nod and unhook wires.

"Call it," says a doctor snapping off his gloves. "What's everyone doing for lunch?"

"11:11 on her."

"I could eat."

2

Remy points to her feet.

Red slush. It flows from Mom's back and oozes off the edges of the table and drips warm on Remy's feet. She's never seen a color so bright. The twin horses appear in the center of the room and tell her it's time to go and she opens her eyes for the last time against Adam's chest and her mouth falls open. Hundred the dog howls from the sidewalk surrounded by cops looking at the sky. Remy taps Adam on his shoulder, who is connected to Mom because he still holds her, he can't let go, and they are connected to Dad who stands on the other side of the bed squeezing Mom's hand and it's true, the sun is here.

On an overcast Wednesday afternoon, Patrick N. Allen took his own life. He is survived by his father, Patrick, Sr.; his step-mother, Patricia; his step-sister, Patty; and his twin brother, Seth.

Coming 2015

Written & Directed by Eric Obenauf

Part-thriller, part-nightmarish examination of the widening gap between originality and technology, told with remarkable precision. Haunting and engaging, *The Removals* imagines where we go from here.

Coming 2015

Written by Nicholas Rombes
Directed by Grace Krilanovich

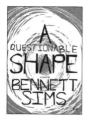

Also published by **TWO DOLLAR RADIO**

NOTHING
A NOVEL BY ANNE MARIE WIRTH CAUCHON

"Apocalyptic and psychologically attentive. I was moved."
—Tao Lin, *New York Times Book Review*

"A riveting first piece of scripture from our newest prophet of misspent youth." —*Paste*

"The energy almost makes each page glow. Though this novel starts as Bret Easton Ellis, it ends as Nick Cave – thunderous, apocalyptic." —*Electric Literature's 'The Outlet'*

SEVEN DAYS IN RIO
A NOVEL BY FRANCIS LEVY

"The funniest American novel since Sam Lipsyte's *The Ask*."
—*Village Voice*

"Like an erotic version of Luis Bunuel's *The Discreet Charm of the Bourgeoisie*." —*The Cult*

MADE TO BREAK
A NOVEL BY D. FOY

"With influences that range from Jack Kerouac to Tom Waits and a prose that possesses a fast, strange, perennially changing rhythm that's somewhat akin to some of John Coltrane's wildest compositions." —*HTML Giant*

"Strange and freewheeling... cerebral and immediate."
—*Los Angeles Review of Books*

THE CAVE MAN
A NOVEL BY XIAODA XIAO

✱ *WOSU* (NPR member station) Favorite Book of 2009.

"As a parable of modern China, [*The Cave Man*] is chilling."
—*Boston Globe*

Also published by **TWO DOLLAR RADIO**

CRAPALACHIA
A NOVEL BY SCOTT MCCLANAHAN

"[McClanahan] aims to lasso the moon... He is not a writer of half-measures. The man has purpose. This is his symphony, every note designed to resonate, to linger." —*New York Times Book Review*

"*Crapalachia* is the genuine article: intelligent, atmospheric, raucously funny and utterly wrenching. McClanahan joins Daniel Woodrell and Tom Franklin as a master chronicler of backwoods rural America." —*The Washington Post*

RADIO IRIS
A NOVEL BY ANNE-MARIE KINNEY

"Kinney is a Southern California Camus." —*Los Angeles Magazine*

"[*Radio Iris*] has a dramatic otherworldly payoff that is unexpected and triumphant." —*New York Times Book Review*, Editors' Choice

THE PEOPLE WHO WATCHED HER PASS BY
A NOVEL BY SCOTT BRADFIELD

"Challenging [and] original... A billowy adventure of a book. In a book that supplies few answers, Bradfield's lavish eloquence is the presiding constant." —*New York Times Book Review*

"Brave and unforgettable. Scott Bradfield creates a country for the reader to wander through, holding Sal's hand, assuming goodness." —*Los Angeles Times*

I'M TRYING TO REACH YOU
A NOVEL BY BARBARA BROWNING

✱ *The Believer* Book Award Finalist

"I think I love this book so much because it contains intimations of the potential of what books can be in the future, and also because it's hilarious." —Emily Gould, *BuzzFeed*

NOG
A NOVEL BY RUDOLPH WURLITZER

"[*Nog*'s] combo of Samuel Beckett syntax and hippie-era freakiness mapped out new literary territory for generations to come." —*Time Out New York*

THE DROP EDGE OF YONDER
A NOVEL BY RUDOLPH WURLITZER

✱ *Time Out New York*'s Best Book of 2008.
✱ *ForeWord* Magazine 2008 Gold Medal in Literary Fiction.
"A picaresque American *Book of the Dead*... in the tradition of Thomas Pynchon, Joseph Heller, Kurt Vonnegut, and Terry Southern." —*Los Angeles Times*

FLATS / QUAKE
TWO CLASSIC NOVELS BY RUDOLPH WURLITZER

"Wurlitzer might be the closest thing we have to an actual cult author, a highly talented fiction writer."
—*Barnes & Noble Review*

"Together they provide a tour of the dissolution of identity that was daily life in the sixties."
—Michael Silverblatt, *KCRW's Bookworm*

DAMASCUS
A NOVEL BY JOSHUA MOHR

"*Damascus* succeeds in conveying a big-hearted vision."
—*The Wall Street Journal*

"Nails the atmosphere of a San Francisco still breathing in the smoke that lingers from the days of Jim Jones and Dan White." —*New York Times Book Review*

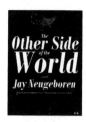

Also published by **TWO DOLLAR RADIO**

1940
A NOVEL BY JAY NEUGEBOREN

❋ Long list, 2010 International IMPAC Dublin Literary Award.

"Jay Neugeboren traverses the Hitlerian tightrope with all the skill and formal daring that have made him one of our most honored writers of literary fiction and masterful nonfiction."
— *Los Angeles Times*

TERMITE PARADE
A NOVEL BY JOSHUA MOHR

❋ *Sacramento Bee* Best Read of 2010.

"[A] wry and unnerving story of bad love gone rotten. [Mohr] has a generous understanding of his characters, whom he describes with an intelligence and sensitivity that pulls you in. This is no small achievement." —*New York Times Book Review*

I SMILE BACK
A NOVEL BY AMY KOPPELMAN

"Powerful. Koppelman's instincts help her navigate these choppy waters with inventiveness and integrity." —*Los Angeles Times*

EROTOMANIA: A ROMANCE
A NOVEL BY FRANCIS LEVY

❋ *Queerty* Top 10 Book of 2008.
❋ *Inland Empire Weekly* Standout Book of 2008.

"Miller, Lawrence, and Genet stop by like proud ancestors."
—*Village Voice*